D1461013

Sneezing Powder

and

Other Stories

by
ENID BLYTON

Illustrated by
Ray Mutimer

AWARD PUBLICATIONS LIMITED

For further information on Enid Blyton please contact
www.blyton.com

ISBN 0-86163-932-4

This compilation text copyright © 1998 The Enid Blyton Company
Illustrations copyright © 1998 Award Publications Limited

Enid Blyton's signature is a trademark of
The Enid Blyton Company

This edition entitled *Sneezing Powder and Other Stories*
published by permission of The Enid Blyton Company

First published 1998
4th impression 2002

Published by Award Publications Limited,
27 Longford street, London NW1 3DZ

Printed in Singapore

CONTENTS

Sneezing Powder

Once upon a time there lived a brownie called Smarty. He kept a little shop in Hallo Town, in which he sold jars of honey, fine yellow lemons, and big yellow pills that helped to cure colds.

In the wintertime Smarty did a fine trade, for anyone who had a cold came to buy his honey, his juicy lemons, and his cold-pills. Then they would go home, squeeze the lemons into a glass, put in hot water and sugar and a spoonful or two of Smarty's golden honey, take a cold-pill, and go to bed – and lo and behold, next morning they were cured!

But in the summertime nobody seemed to have a cold at all. It was most annoying for Smarty. Instead of thinking of selling something else, such as ice creams or cool lemon drinks, Smarty still went on hoping that people would have colds and buy his cold-cure. So he wasn't quite as smart as his name, was he?

He was quite smart enough to think out a naughty trick, though!

"If only I could make people think they had a cold, they would come and buy my honey and lemons and pills," thought Smarty. "If only they would sneeze or cough just as they passed my shop, it would be so easy for me to say, 'Dear me! You are getting a cold! Buy my cold-cure before you are very bad!' But nobody ever sneezes outside my shop."

Smarty sat and thought for a bit, and then he grinned all over his sly little face. He slapped his knee in delight. He had thought of a wonderful idea!

"I'll go and buy some sneezing powder from old Dame Flap!" he said to himself. "And I'll put some into my pepperpot and shake it out of my bedroom window whenever anyone passes! Then they will sneeze hard and perhaps come and buy my goods."

So off he went to buy the sneezing powder. He paid Dame Flap a silver coin for a boxful and she wrapped it up for him. It was a strange powder, rather like fine green flour, and it had a strange smell.

Smarty ran home with it. He emptied some into his pepperpot and slipped upstairs to his bedroom window, which was just over his shop. He leaned out in excitement. Was anybody coming?

Yes – here was Old Man Shuffle! Smarty waited till he was underneath the window and then he shook out some of the powder. It went on Old Man Shuffle's nose, and he stopped. He took out his big blue handkerchief and held it to his nose.

"Whooosh!" he sneezed. "A-whoosh!"

"Hi, Old Man Shuffle, you've got a dreadful cold!" called Smarty. "Come into my shop and get some honey and lemons and pills!"

So in shuffled the old fellow, thinking it was very lucky that he should be outside Smarty's shop just when his cold had begun. He bought a jar of honey, two lemons, and a box of yellow pills. Smarty grinned. He ran up to his bedroom again.

"Ah! Here are Mr Twiddle and his wife!" chuckled Smarty. He shook his pepperpot over them. They stopped and fumbled for their hankies.

"Er-tish-oo!" said Mr Twiddle loudly.

"Ish-ish-ish!" sneezed Mrs Twiddle politely into her handkerchief.

"ER-TISH-OOO!" went Mr Twiddle.

"Not so much noise, Twiddle," said Mrs Twiddle. "Ish-ish-ish-ish! Dear me! We are beginning colds, I think. Look, let's buy some honey and lemons, and maybe we'll stop our colds from getting worse."

So into Smarty's shop they went and bought what they wanted, much to

Smarty's delight. As soon as they had gone, he popped upstairs again with his pepperpot full of sneezing powder.

He made Twinkle the pixie sneeze and buy honey and pills. He made Mr Meddle sneeze so strongly that his hat flew on to the roof and he had to get a ladder to fetch it. He made Dame Winks sneeze twelve times, and at the end her bonnet was right over her nose and she couldn't see where she was going at all.

Oh, Smarty had plenty of fun that day, and he made plenty of money too! But when everyone found that they had no cold at all when they got home, and didn't need the honey and lemons, they were rather puzzled. They talked about it to one another, and they found that all of them had begun their sneezing fits outside Smarty's shop.

"Very nice for Smarty!" said Mr Meddle. "Let us go along and see what we can see."

So they all went back toward Smarty's shop, and peeped round the corner. And they saw Smarty leaning out of his

bedroom window, pepperpot in hand!

"Aha!" Old Man Shuffle said angrily. "So that's his trick, is it! Come along everybody!"

They all went into Smarty's shop. Smarty hurried down to serve them. Mrs Twiddle was waiting for him. She snatched the pepperpot out of his pocket and shook it all over Smarty.

"Colds are catching today!" she said.

"Sneeze, Smarty, sneeze! Dear, dear! You must have caught our colds."

"Whoosh!" said Smarty. "Atish-o! Ish-ish-ish! Osha-whoosh! Tish-oo!"

Mrs Twiddle emptied all the sneezing powder over him. My goodness, Smarty simply could not stop sneezing! It was dreadful!

"By the time you've finished I guess you'll want to buy a pot of your own honey, a dozen lemons, and a box of pills!" said Mr Twiddle, laughing. "Goodbye, Smarty. It serves you right!"

They all went out, giggling and chuckling, and they could hear Smarty's sneezes all the way down the road.

Poor Smarty! He sneezed all that day and all that night, and by that time his nose and throat and eyes were so sore that he had to take two jars of honey, six lemons, and two of his own pills to cure himself!

Now he has shut up his shop and gone out selling ice creams. And a very much better idea, too, in the summer – don't you think so?

You're
Late!

"Bessie, the words I say to you more often than any others are – 'You're late!'" said Mother. "Why must you always be late? Are you lazy, or slow, or what is it?"

"I don't know," said Bessie.

"You're late for breakfast, and if I didn't hurry you off each day for school, you'd be late there, and you're always home late for lunch and tea," said her mother.

"Why bother about her?" said Granny. "Why not let her be late? You don't need to wait breakfast or lunch or tea – and surely her teacher at school can punish her if she's late. Why bother?"

"Well – that doesn't seem a bad idea!" said Mother. "I'm getting so tired of saying 'You're late, you're late, you're

14

late!' I hate nagging. I won't say it any more. Bessie, you can be as late as you like, but we just shan't wait for you, that's all."

Bessie thought it would be nice not to be grumbled at any more. She ate her tea, and then went to do her homework.

"When you've done that, would you like to catch the bus with me?" asked Granny. "I've got a new book at home for you, and you can fetch it and then catch the bus back."

"Oh yes, Granny," said Bessie, pleased. Granny always chose lovely books for her. Perhaps it would be an adventure story – or a book about the Faraway Tree. Lovely!

"I'll start at six o'clock," said Granny, and didn't say any more. Bessie finished her homework. It was twenty to six. Lots of time before Granny went.

She went into the garden to play with Spanker the dog. They had a fine game, and then Bessie went indoors again. There was no sign of either her mother or Granny.

She pulled on her coat and ran into the street. The bus was at the corner – and there was Granny getting into it!

"Wait, wait!" shouted Bessie. But the

bus didn't wait. Mother waved goodbye to Granny and then turned to go home. She almost bumped into Bessie.

"Oh, Mummy, why didn't you tell me it was getting late!" said Bessie, almost in tears.

"Well, you know I'm not going to bother you any more," said her mother. "Now don't cry about it. It's not my fault or Granny's. It's your own."

Bessie was very upset. She wanted to catch the next bus, but Mother said no. So she had to go home.

When she went up to bed, her mother kissed her goodnight, but she didn't say "Now, hurry up" or "Don't be late for breakfast." She just said, "Sleep well, dear."

Bessie dawdled as usual. Nobody shouted up to her to hurry or she'd be late to bed. But after about half an hour her father came up and went into the bathroom.

Bessie hadn't had her bath. She went into the bathroom. "Oh Daddy – I haven't had my bath yet."

17

"Why not?" said Father. "You've been up here for ages! I want the bathroom now. You will have to go without your bath. Sorry!"

"Bother!" said Bessie, and went to bed without the warm bath she loved.

Mother tapped on her door in the morning, "Half past seven, Bessie!"

Bessie turned over and went to sleep again. Her mother didn't come and rout her out as she usually did. She didn't even call up the stairs. So Bessie slept on.

She didn't get up until half past eight. Breakfast was at eight o'clock, so you can see how late she was. She flung on her clothes, forgot to wash, or to clean her teeth, drew a comb through her hair and ran downstairs. There was no breakfast on the table! The cloth was off, and the pot of flowers stood in the centre. What had happened?

"Mummy! Where's breakfast?" cried Bessie. "I'm in an awful hurry."

Her mother didn't say "You're late." She just put her head into the dining-room and said, "Breakfast? Oh, we had

18

that at eight o'clock. I've cleared it away now. I can't start cooking again. If you want anything, cut yourself some bread and butter."

"But it's time I went to school," said Bessie, almost crying.

"I'm sorry, dear," said Mother. "But it's not my fault. I'm quite determined not to keep nagging you about being late."

Bessie had to cut herself some bread and butter, and put some marmalade on it. That was all she had for her breakfast. Then she rushed off to school. But she was late, of course.

"Bessie! Stay in at playtime," said Miss Brown, crossly. "And good gracious, child, haven't you washed or done your hair this morning? Go to the cloakroom at once. You are a dreadful sight. Why, half your buttons are undone. I'm ashamed of you."

The other girls giggled at Bessie. She

went red and fled to the cloakroom to wash and do her hair. She had to stay in at playtime and write out *I must not be late* fifty times.

On the way home to lunch she saw some men laying some big drainpipes at the side of the road. She stopped to watch them. Then she saw some exciting looking puzzles in the toyshop and spent ten minutes making up her mind which one to buy next time she had any money.

Well, Bessie always did dawdle home, so this was nothing new. She was always late for lunch, and Mother usually greeted her with "You're late, Bessie!"

But this time she didn't. She was sitting having her lunch, all by herself, reading a book. She had some stewed apple and custard on her plate. She looked up as Bessie came in.

"Hello, Bessie. Have a good morning, dear?"

"Not very," said Bessie, rather sulkily. "I was late for school. Miss Brown was very cross, and I had to stay in at playtime."

"Well, I expect you will tomorrow, too," said her mother. "Still, you'll probably get used to it, won't you."

"I shan't be late tomorrow," said Bessie. "I won't have the girls laughing at me again as they did this morning. Horrid things!"

"Sit down and have some apple and custard," said Mother.

"Where's the meat?" asked Bessie, in surprise. "I thought you said that we were going to have cold meat and potatoes in their jackets and tomatoes today for our lunch."

"Yes, I did have that," said Mother. "But I didn't wait for you. I didn't know how late you would be. I had mine at quarter past one as usual. It's nearly quarter to two now. The first course is all cleared away."

"Am I only to have my pudding, then?" asked Bessie, ready to burst into tears. "I hardly had any breakfast!"

"I'm sorry, dear – but it wasn't my fault," said her mother. "Eat up your apple and custard. I told you I wasn't

22

going to nag at you, or wait for you any more. You must come in as late as you please, but don't expect me to keep things hot for you."

Bessie ate her pudding, and sniffed miserably. Mother took no notice. She looked at the clock once, but she didn't say a word to Bessie. Bessie had a music lesson at a quarter past two. Well, well – she must be late for it, that's all!

And she was! She was ten minutes late, and when she got there she found her music teacher in a great rage, for

he was a hot-tempered man.

"You have kept me waiting for ten minutes, ten whole minutes!" he almost shouted at her when she went into the room. "What impertinence! I shall report you to the headmistress. Why did your mother not send you in time?"

Bessie said nothing. She could not tell this angry music teacher that her mother was tired of telling her to hurry up or she would be late. She went red and looked down.

"You cannot even say you are sorry, I suppose?" said the music teacher. "Now we will have no pieces at all today – you have wasted the time we could have spent on your pretty pieces. We will have only scales and arpeggios!"

How dull! But the teacher would not let her play anything else at all. He was very cross indeed.

You will be surprised to hear that Bessie got home in very good time for tea! You see, she was so very hungry by that time that she simply flew home for her tea. She even laid the table for her

mother, so that she could have it more
quickly.

"Good gracious, Bessie!" said her
mother, looking quite pleased, "you are
home nice and early – and it's such a
help if you lay the table."

Bessie felt happier. She ate an
enormous tea, and then actually helped
to wash up. Then she did her homework.
She looked at the clock. There was a Girl
Guide meeting at six. She was a guide,
and she wanted to go.

But at six she hadn't even changed
into her Guide uniform! There she was,
reading hard. Mother didn't say a word.

She just went on with her knitting.

At half past six Bessie looked at the clock. "Gracious! Look at the time! Oh, Mummy, by the time I've changed and got to the meeting it will be over. And we were going to have such fun tonight. The Captain won't be at all pleased with me for not going."

"I expect she will be most disappointed in you," said Mother. "You've always gone before because I've managed to get you off in time. What a pity!"

Bessie was cross. Why couldn't her mother have reminded her? This was a silly trick she was playing. Bessie went out into the garden and sat down in the shed. Now she had missed the meeting. Bother, bother, blow!

She began to mess about in the shed. She heard the supper bell ring, and began to tidy up all the things she had muddled. Then she found a flower catalogue and couldn't help looking at it. Oh, what lovely flowers people could buy for their gardens! When she was old enough she would buy this – and that – and that . . .

"Gracious! I forgot about supper!" she said suddenly, and tore indoors. She popped her head in at the dining-room. Father was there, having his supper with Mother. Bessie took a hurried look at the table. Poached eggs! Ooooh!

She flew upstairs to wash her hands, do her hair and put on a clean dress. Alas, when she got down again, supper was over and Mother was clearing away. Bessie burst into angry tears.

Her father spoke to her sternly.

"If you want to make a scene and a noise, you can – but not down here. Go and howl in your bedroom. It's your own fault if you've missed your supper. You heard the bell. You'll probably miss breakfast tomorrow, too, and no doubt have to go without a bath again. Well, Mummy and I are just not going to hurry you up any more. Go and think about it a little."

Bessie went upstairs crying. She sat down on the bed. She had wanted to yell and stamp and make a fuss downstairs, just to upset her mother. But up here, all alone, it would be silly to do that. There was nobody to see, nobody to mind at all.

She sat and thought hard. A few tears trickled down her face again. "I don't think Daddy and Mummy love me any more," she said. "They're tired of me! I wonder if they'll like me any better if I do try to be punctual and help a bit more. I'm always so late that I can never even help to lay the table."

She dried her eyes and went downstairs. "Mummy," she said, in a forlorn kind of voice, "I don't think you like me very much, or Daddy either. But I'm going to try and be better. Please love me again!"

"My dear child, of course we love you," said her father. "But I can't say I have liked you very much lately. We shall always love you – but it would be so nice to like you, too. We shall, if you

try to help in every way you can."

"Then I will," said Bessie. "I really will. And I'll begin by hurrying up when I go to bed, so that I can have a bath before you want to get into the bathroom, Daddy!"

And you'll hardly believe it, but Bessie really was different from that very evening. Down to breakfast in time, off to school early, back home early, and never once did her mother say again "You're late, Bessie!"

You know, it was really a very good idea of her granny's to tell her mother to stop saying hurry up, she was late, wasn't it? All the same, I hope your mother doesn't play the same trick on you!

The
Runaway Hen

"I'm just going to take Diana Susan for a ride in her pram, Mummy!" called Beth. "I won't be long. I'm only going down the end of the lane and back again."

"Well, post this letter for me, darling," said her mother, and Beth took it and slipped it under Diana Susan's pillow. Then off she went, out of the gate and down the lane.

She heard the cluck-luck-lucking of Mrs Dawkins' hens next door, and wondered if one of them had laid an egg. What a lot of cackling was going on! She peeped through the hedge to see why.

Goodness – there was a dog chasing the hens – and one hen was racing up the garden as fast as she could go with the dog after her. It was only a puppy,

31

and meant to have a game, but the hen didn't know that! It fled out of the gate and ran down the lane.

"Puppy! Stop that!" shouted Beth. "What's your name now? I've forgotten. Oh yes – Tinker. Come here, Tinker. It's very, very bad to chase hens. You'll get into trouble if you do things like that. Go home!" and she pointed sternly down the road.

Tinker put his tail down and ran off at once. He knew quite well he had done wrong.

"It's all right, hens, he's gone!" Beth called through the hedge. Then she remembered the hen that had run down the lane. Had she better tell Mrs Dawkins about it? No, perhaps she had better see if she could find the hen. So down the lane she went, wheeling Diana Susan in her lovely blue pram, keeping her eyes open for the hen.

She couldn't see it anywhere. Whatever could have happened to it? Then she saw it, still running fast, going towards the main road. Beth called to it.

"Hen! Don't go there! There are cars whizzing along at sixty miles an hour! Come back, hen!"

But the hen took no notice at all. It was quite lost, it was afraid that the puppy was still chasing it, and it meant to run and run and run!

"Oh, you silly little hen," said Beth, pushing her pram as fast as she could. "If only you'd come back this way I could get behind you and shoo you home."

The hen still ran on and on, and at last came to the main road. A car whizzed by so quickly that the poor hen had quite a shock. She thought it must be a very big puppy.

Then another car came by, saw the hen and hooted at it.

The hen scuttled into the hedge. Yes, that must have been another puppy, because it said "parp-parp", and sounded very like the puppy's barking. The hen peered out of the hedge, wondering if it could make a dash for the other side of the road. Perhaps it would find the other hens there. It really didn't know where it was at all!

Just as Beth came up to where the lane met the main road the hen made a dash across it. A car whizzed by at the same moment, just avoiding the hen, but frightening it very much indeed. It sank down at the side of the road and drooped its head on to its chest. Beth left her pram and hurried over to the hen.

"Are you hurt?" she said. "Or just very frightened? Oh, you poor creature, you do look ill! Can you walk? If you can, I'll guide you home."

But the hen couldn't walk. It had had such a scare that it couldn't even stand. It just lay there, looking very feathery and floppy, its eyes half closed.

35

"I'll carry you safely across, back to my pram," said Beth, and picked the hen up in her arms. It felt quite heavy. It gave a feeble cluck and then lay quite still. Beth carried it over the road to her pram.

"I don't know what to do with you," she said. "You can't walk. And I can't carry you all the way home and wheel my pram too. Well – I hope my doll won't mind, but I'm afraid you'll have to ride in the pram too, hen!"

Beth moved her doll to one side and put the hen into the pram. It didn't seem to mind at all. It gave another little cluck and then settled down in a big feathery heap. The doll looked surprised, but she didn't seem to mind either.

"Now, I'll wheel you home, so please be sensible and don't fly out of the pram," said Beth, and she began to push the pram slowly back down the lane.

The hen shut its eyes and seemed to go to sleep. A man came hurrying by on his way to catch the bus and he was most astonished to see a hen in a doll's pram.

He simply couldn't understand it, but he didn't say anything about it because he was already late for the bus.

When Beth came near to her own front gate she saw her mother there talking to Mrs Dawkins, who had just come back from doing her shopping in the village.

"Oh, there you are, Beth," said her mother. "Have you had a – why . . . good gracious me! *Whatever* have you got in your pram, Beth?"

"A hen!" said Mrs Dawkins. "And it

looks like one of mine. Well I never! Do you usually take my hens for rides in your pram, Beth?"

"Oh no. But a puppy chased the hens," explained Beth. "And this one was frightened and ran down the lane to the main road. A car nearly ran over it and it felt ill, so I put it into my pram to bring it back home. I do hope it isn't hurt."

Mrs Dawkins lifted it out and looked at it carefully. It suddenly opened its wings and flung itself out of Mrs Dawkins'

arms. It ran to join the others. "Not much wrong with it," said Mrs Dawkins, laughing. "Well, you are kind, Beth, to bring my hen home."

"Did you post my letter, dear?" asked Beth's mother.

"Oh dear – no!" said Beth. "The hen made me forget." She groped under the doll's pillow for the letter, and then gave a squeal of surprise. "Here's the letter – and something else as well. Oh *look*!" And she brought out a big brown egg and the letter too. How her mother and Mrs Dawkins laughed.

"Well! It wanted to give you a present for helping it," said Mrs Dawkins. "You must have that for your breakfast. I'm sure it will taste very good!"

It did, and Beth enjoyed it very much. It was nice of the hen, wasn't it? It sometimes lays an egg under the hedge between Mrs Dawkins' garden and Beth's and then Mrs Dawkins says Beth must have it, because she is sure that the hen means it for her. I expect she does, too!

Aha,
Mister Rat!

Mister Rat was a horrid fellow, cruel and cunning. He was always hungry, and he loved to find the nests of the birds and eat their eggs or young ones; he loved to sniff out the nests of the little dormice and gobble up their babies; he would even pounce on a young rabbit if it was all alone.

Mowdie the mole walked along the bottom of the ditch, weeping. She did not often walk above ground, for she loved to tunnel below the earth – but this morning she forgot about burrowing and scuffed along in the ditch.

"What is the matter?" asked Bobtail the rabbit, putting her pretty head out of a hole nearby.

"Oh, oh, Mister Rat has found my nest

40

in the field," wept Mowdie the mole. "And he has eaten all my new little babies, he hasn't left me even one!"

"The wicked fellow!" said Bobtail, her nose woffling up and down. "It is time he was punished!"

"He should be eaten up himself!" said Spiky the hedgehog, uncurling himself where he lay at the bottom of the ditch. "I would eat him myself if I could find him! Yes, I would!"

There came the sound of a laugh in the hedge and all three creatures stiffened with fear. They knew that squealing laugh – it was the snicker of the rat himself!

"So you would eat me yourself, would you?" said Mister Rat, putting his long nose out of the hedge. "Come along then, Spiky – come and eat me – or you, Bobtail – or you, Mowdie Mole! I'm here!"

Bobtail the rabbit disappeared down her hole. Mowdie the mole dug a tunnel in the ditch and sank into it as quick as lightning. Spiky the hedgehog curled himself up tightly and lay there quite still. The rat ran out and sniffed at him.

"You would not be so bold if you hadn't your armour of prickles!" he said to the hedgehog. "I will go and tell the fox to come and get you!"

He ran off. Spiky was full of fear. He did not like the fox, because Reynard could make Spiky uncurl by making himself smell so horrid that, in disgust, the hedgehog felt he must crawl away! And, as soon as he uncurled himself to crawl away from Reynard's dreadful smell, the fox would seize him!

Spiky hurried away and hid himself in a hole in the bank. It was only just big enough for him, and had a ferny

curtain hiding the entrance. He felt safe
there.

Mister Rat snickered softly to himself
as he ran about the hedge and slunk over
the fields. He was king of the countryside! He was lord of all the creatures
of the hedge and ditch! Soon there
would be dozens more rats, for in nests
here and there young ones were growing
up. Aha! Mister Rat would teach them
how to hunt for the nests of young mice,

for the soft-spined young hedgehogs, for the nestlings in the hedges, for the lizards that darted about the sunny side of the bank and even for the frogs that lived in the long green grass by the pond.

Mister Rat was very fond of eggs. He had sucked dozens that he had found in nests in the hedgerow. He knew how to glance upwards as he ran along the hedge bank, and spy nests cleverly hidden here and there. Then up he would climb, stick his sharp grey nose into the nest and gobble up the eggs there. Many a robin, thrush, and blackbird had come back in haste to her nest and had found all her eggs gone.

Mister Rat even went down to the farm and stole the eggs in the hen-house. He had many ways of doing that. He would slink in to the house through a hole he knew well, and suck an egg in the nesting box. He would perhaps take one away with him too, to store it in his hole. How he managed to get it out of the nest without breaking it was marvellous! Then he would roll it over and

over to the hole he had entered by. He would push it through this hole and then roll the egg to his nest. Sometimes two rats stole the eggs together. Then one would turn on his back and hold the egg, and the other would pull him along. Ah, Mister Rat was the cleverest creature in the kingdom!

But one day he made a great mistake.

He was looking out for eggs as usual. He had eaten two belonging to the hedge-sparrow. They were as blue as the sky, but very small. The rat swallowed them but still felt hungry. He wondered if there were any eggs hidden in the ash tree that stood at the corner of the field. He knew it was partly hollow inside. Once a squirrel had nested there. Then Mister Rat had had a fine feast of young squirrels!

Once a woodpecker had nested there, and Mister Rat had eaten every egg she had laid, till, in despair, she left the tree and flew away to the pinewood on the hill.

Yes – Mister Rat would see if any bird had nested in the ash tree this year! He ran to it, slinking along in the nettles that grew in the ditch. He climbed nimbly up the trunk. It was night-time, but the moon was out, and Mister Rat could see quite well. He came to the entrance of the hole. He sat there and sniffed.

Yes! Some bird was nesting there! The nest smelled of bird. Mister Rat caught sight of something white in the hole. An egg. He slipped down and got it. It was good! But only one egg! How

46

disappointing! Never mind, perhaps there would be others in a day or two.

There were! In two days there was another egg. Mister Rat ate that. In a week's time there was another. Mister Rat ate that! Four days after that there was another – and Mister Rat had that too.

Now the bird who owned the hole in the ash tree that year was a little owl. She was puzzled to find that her eggs disappeared so mysteriously. She was a young little owl and had never laid eggs before. She told her mate about it, and he hissed solemnly.

"Someone has been stealing them," he said. "Maybe it is the grey squirrel. He is a robber. Or maybe it is the thieving jackdaw. He loves other birds' eggs. We will find out."

It was the dormouse who told the little owl who the robber was.

"It is Mister Rat," said the quivering dormouse, from the shelter of the hedge. "Do not catch me, little owl, for I came to warn you of the robber. He stole my own little ones before they even had their eyes open. No one is safe – not even you, little owl!"

The little owls hissed angrily. So that was the robber who had stolen their eggs. This must be seen to.

"Are there many rats here?" said the owls.

"Oh, very many," answered the frightened dormouse. "His families are all growing well now – soon there will be a hundred and more rats running about here and we will all have to flee away. But they will follow us, so we shall be no better off!"

The owls hissed again and flew away. They knew what they were going to do. They flew to the big wood five miles away. Here many little owls nested and brought up their young ones – but lately there had been too little food for them, because the weasels had been about and eaten much of the food that the little owls wanted for their youngsters.

The two little owls called their friends. "Wee-oo, wee-oo, koo-wee-oo!" they called. "Koo-wee-oo!"

"Tvit, tvit!" answered their friends, and from far and near the little owls flew down to the tree where sat the two who had come from the faraway wood.

"Wee-oo, wee-oo!" said the two owls. "We come to tell you of much food in a wood far off. Bring your little ones there as soon as they are grown. There are rats by the score in the wood we know."

"We will come!" cried the owls. "Tvit, tvit!" And in three weeks' time, when the young rats were half grown, and were filling the countryside with fear and panic, a great flock of little owls came

to the wood nearby. With them they
brought their half-fledged youngsters,
still downy – but with claws that could
shut like a trap!

"Wee-oo, wee-oo!" called the little owls,
as they flew about the wood. They saw
the grass move a little in the pale
moonlight – down swept an owl, and
fixed a young rat in its claws. The rat
squealed but could not get away. Another
owl dropped like a stone on to a full-
grown rat and it had not even time to
squeal.

"Tvit, tvit! We have feasted well!" cried

the owls that night, as they flew to trees to hide away for the daytime.

Mister Rat was scared to find that so many owls were about. But he said to himself, "Am I not king of the countryside, and lord of the hedgerow? I am afraid of nobody!"

He had a fine wife, and she had a litter of seven small rats that Mister Rat was proud of. His wife would only let him peep at them, for she was afraid he might eat them. Rats did eat their own children sometimes, she knew. Mister Rat ran to warn her to keep close-hidden.

The next night a little owl saw a movement in the grass near the pond.

He pounced – and there was a scuffle! He had caught the mother-rat – and nearby in the hole he could hear the little ones squealing! He hooted to his comrades and they flew down and ate up all the young rats.

And then it was Mister Rat who ran along the ditch wailing and weeping for his lost family. But no one heeded him or comforted him. The rabbit was glad. The mole laughed. The hedgehog grunted and said to himself, "Do as you would be done by, Mister Rat! You are being served in the same way as you served us!"

There was a squeal in the night. A little owl had caught Mister Rat himself! Ah, Mister Rat, that's the end of you!

"So it was you who ate all my eggs, was it!" cried the little owl, as she held Mister Rat in her sharp claws.

"Let me go and I'll never do such a thing again!" squealed the frightened rat.

"You will never do such a thing again anyhow!" said the owl, eating him up.

That was the end of Mister Rat – and as for the few rats that were left they fled from that part of the country in terror. And now the rabbit, the mole, the mice and the hedgehogs go about in peace and happiness. Aha, Mister Rat, you were a bit too clever when you ate the eggs of the little owl!

The Big
Humming-Top

Once upon a time there was a big humming-top. It was as tall as the biggest doll in the nursery, and as fat as two teddy bears put together – so you can guess what a big one it was!

It was shining silver, with a handle of red wood. When the handle was pressed down two or three times the top spun round and round on the floor, making a most wonderful humming noise – like this – Ooooomooooooooomoooooom!

The humming-top had a great friend, and that was Whiskers the cat. None of the other toys liked Whiskers because he could walk so quietly on his velvet pads that he very often made them jump. Also one day he had scratched the monkey, quite by mistake.

So the toys thought that the humming-top was wrong to make friends with Whiskers, and they didn't have very much to do with him. This hurt his feelings rather, because he was a friendly top and liked to talk to others. But it is very hard to talk to people who turn their backs on you and whistle when you speak to them – and that is what the rude monkey often did when the humming-top spoke to him.

One night an awful thing happened. A gnome came into the playroom through the window, and what do you think he did? He went straight to the toy sweet-shop and stole a bottle of little

sweets! Yes, he did – took it right off the shelf, and ran off with it!

Well, the toys were very shocked and very angry. They all gathered together and talked about it.

"When Jane and Leslie come into the playroom tomorrow morning, they will see that one of their bottles of sweets is gone, and they will perhaps think that one of us toys took it!" said the big doll.

"How dreadful!" cried everyone, looking quite pale with horror. "Let's think what we can do to stop the gnome stealing any more!"

But, you know, they simply couldn't think of any way to stop him. The humming-top tried to speak once or twice, but the toys wouldn't listen to him. They just turned their backs on him as usual.

Now the next night the gnome came back again – and he took a little bottle of peppermints! Fancy that! Yes, in spite of all the toys rushing at him to stop him, he managed to get it and run off with it! He pushed the monkey over and trod on the biggest doll's toes. Oh, he was a rough fellow!

The toys were in tears. This was dreadful. Whatever were they to do?

The humming-top spoke loudly.

"If you will allow me to tell my friend Whiskers, the cat, I think perhaps I can find some way of frightening that robber gnome," he said.

"Pooh!" said the toys scornfully. "If we can't think of an idea, a cat won't be able to, that's certain."

"But Whiskers is very clever," said the top. "He might even come and hide here in the playroom at night."

"That wouldn't be any good!" said the monkey. "You know quite well that the gnome would smell him as soon as he got to the window! Gnomes have noses as sharp as dogs!"

The humming-top said no more – but when the gnome came again and took a third bottle of sweets, he made up his mind to talk to Whiskers at once.

Whiskers listened patiently, and when he heard how the gnome had taken the

bottles he swung his tail from side to side angrily.

"It's no good me hiding in the room," he said, "because the gnome would smell me there. If only there was some way of letting me know as soon as the gnome appears! I sleep in the kitchen, but as soon as I knew the gnome was in the playroom it wouldn't take me two seconds to come flying up the stairs to catch him!"

The top thought for a moment, and then he had an idea.

"Could you hear me hum if I hummed

in the playroom and you were in the
kitchen?" he asked.

"Easily!" answered the cat.

"Well!" said the top, eagerly, "I'll tell
you what I'll do – I'll get the monkey to
spin me as soon as the gnome comes,
and as I spin I'll hum my very loudest,
and you'll hear me. Then you can come
rushing up the stairs!"

"Good!" said Whiskers and purred
loudly. "That's settled then."

The top told the toys his plan. They
didn't think very much of it because they
felt sure the cat wouldn't hear the top
humming. But the monkey promised to
spin the top that night as soon as the
gnome came.

"We'll shut the sweet-shop up tight,
and turn it round towards the wall," said
the top. "The gnome will take a minute
or two more trying to get the sweets then
– and that will give Whiskers just time to
come up the stairs!"

"He won't wake up, you'll see!" said
the big doll.

Well, that night all the toys waited for

the robber to come. They didn't have to wait long. Suddenly he appeared at the window, and jumped lightly down to the floor. He ran over to the toy sweet-shop.

At the same moment the monkey took the big humming-top and pressed the handle up and down three times to make him spin. He spun – and dear

me, you should have heard him hum!
OOOOOOOMOOOOOOOMOOOOOOM
OOOOOOOMOOOOOOOM!

He hummed more loudly than he had ever hummed in his life – and Whiskers the cat, lying asleep in the kitchen, heard the humming and sprang to his feet. In a second he ran up the stairs and burst into the playroom. The gnome had just got the sweet-shop door open and was reaching out his hand for a bottle of peardrops when he saw the cat.

Goodness me, what a shock he got! He ran to the window at once and jumped up on to the sill. Whiskers pounced after him. Out of the window he went, and the cat went out too. All the toys watched in delight.

What a noise there was in the garden! The cat hissed and spat at the gnome and he shouted at her. The toys longed to know what had happened. Presently Whiskers jumped in at the window again, looking very pleased with himself. In his mouth were the three missing bottles of sweets!

"Mew!" said Whiskers, dropping the bottles by the humming-top. "I made that nasty little gnome tell me where he had hidden these bottles and I went to find them! He had only eaten one sweet out of each bottle so there's not much gone. And look! I pulled his red coat off his back!"

The cat dropped a ragged red coat on to the floor, and the toys clapped their hands in glee.

"It serves him right," said Whiskers. "He had no right to come and steal like that. I scratched his shoulder and tore his coat – and I'm sure he won't come again!"

Well, of course, he didn't. He moved from the garden and went five miles away in Tall-Tree Wood. He was so afraid of meeting Whiskers again!

The humming-top was very proud of his friend the cat – and as for the toys they couldn't make enough of the top and the cat. They patted the top and stroked the cat, and said all sorts of nice things.

And now, of course, Whiskers sleeps in the playroom every night with his friends the toys. They love to have him there – and when they want to wake him up for a game they spin the humming-top – OOOOOOOOOOMOOOOOOOOOM OOOOOOOOOOOMMM!

The Little
Sugar House

Mrs Biscuit kept a cake shop in Tweedle Village. All the boys and girls liked her shop because she had such exciting things in the window – gingerbread men, pastry cats and dogs, chocolate horses, and delicious iced cakes.

Mrs Biscuit would have been a very nice woman if only she hadn't told so many stories. She really didn't seem to know how to tell the truth.

"Was this cake baked today?" a customer would ask. "Is it quite fresh?"

"Oh yes, madam, it's just new," Mrs Biscuit would answer, knowing quite well that the cake was stale and dry.

Mrs Biscuit was mean, too. She never gave anything away if she could help it, not even broken bits of stale cake. She made those into puddings for herself.

Now one day she thought she would make a very fine iced cake and put it right in the middle of her window.

"If they come and look at my iced cake they will see my buns, my biscuits, and other things," thought Mrs Biscuit, "and perhaps they will buy them."

So she made a beautiful iced cake with pink roses all round the edge. But she didn't know what to put in the middle.

"I think I'll make a little sugar house," she said to herself. "It shall have windows and a door and two chimneys. Everyone will be delighted to see it."

So she made a wonderful little house all out of sugar. She gave it two red chimneys, four windows, and a little brown door made of chocolate. She put pink sugar roses on the walls, and when it had set hard she popped it on the very top of her big cake. Then she put it into the window.

At first everyone came to look at it but after a little while they thought it was boring.

"Why don't you put someone into your house?" asked a little girl. "Houses are meant to be lived in, aren't they, even sugar houses? Why don't you go to the Very-Little-Goblins and ask one to live in your sugar house? Then people would come every day to see him opening the chocolate door and looking out of the sugar windows at the pink roses."

Well, Mrs Biscuit thought that was a

very good idea. She put on her bonnet and went to where the Very-Little-Goblins lived in their mushroom houses.

"Would one of you like to come and live in a sugar house with pink roses on the walls?" she asked. "It's not like your mushroom houses, up one night and gone the next, so that you have to keep on moving. It stays on my big iced cake for weeks and weeks, and is very beautiful indeed."

The Very-Little-Goblins came out of their mushroom houses and stared at her. "We have heard that you tell stories,"

said their chief goblin. "We are very truthful people, you know, and we couldn't live with anyone who didn't tell the truth."

"Of course I tell the truth!" said Mrs Biscuit, crossly. "Why, I've never told a story in my life!"

"Well, that's splendid," said the chief goblin, quite believing her. "I shall be very pleased to let my eldest son come and live in your little sugar house tomorrow."

"Thank you," said Mrs Biscuit, delighted, and she went home.

Soon everyone knew that one of the Very-Little-Goblins was coming to live on the big iced cake in the window, and all the children of Tweedle Village were tremendously excited.

The next day Twinkle, the Very-Little-Goblin, arrived at Mrs Biscuit's shop. She lifted him up on to the iced cake in the window and showed him the sugar house. He was simply delighted with it.

He opened the little chocolate door and went inside. He had brought no furniture

with him, so he asked Mrs Biscuit if she would make him a little chocolate bed, two sugar chairs, and a chocolate table. He said he would put up curtains at the windows and buy a little carpet for the floor.

Soon the sugar house was quite ready for him, and all the children of the village came to peep at it. It was most exciting to see the goblin open the door and shake his little mats. It was lovely to see him draw the curtains and lean out of the window. Sometimes he would carry his chocolate table and one of his sugar chairs on to the big sugary space outside the little house, and have his lunch there.

Mrs Biscuit did such a lot of trade. A great many people came into the shop to see the iced cake with its sugar house, and of course they had to buy something, so Mrs Biscuit began to be quite rich.

For a little while she remembered to tell the truth to people – and then she forgot.

"Is this chocolate cake fresh?" asked

Dame Tippy one morning.

"Oh yes, quite!" Mrs Biscuit said untruthfully, for the cake had been baked more than a week ago.

"Oh, you storyteller!" cried a tiny voice, and the Very-Little-Goblin peeped out of the sugar house. "You baked that last week."

"Dear, dear, so I did!" Mrs Biscuit said crossly, very angry to hear the goblin's voice. "Take this one instead, Dame Tippy."

The next day a little girl came in for
fresh buns. But Mrs Biscuit quickly
took six stale ones from a tray at the
back of the shop and popped them into
a bag.

"These are nice and new," she said to
the little girl.

"You naughty storyteller! They're as
hard as bricks!" cried the little goblin,
poking his head out of the window of the
sugar house.

"You be quiet! These buns were only
baked this morning," said Mrs Biscuit
angrily.

"Oooh, the storyteller! Oh, little girl,
don't give her your money. She's telling
you stories!"

The little girl ran out of the shop with
her money in her hand, but Mrs Biscuit
called her back.

"I'm only joking with you," she said
to the child. "See, here are some lovely
new buns I baked early this morning."

"Yes, take those," cried the goblin.
"They're all right."

When the little girl had gone, Mrs

Biscuit turned to grumble at the goblin. To her surprise he was rolling up his carpet and taking down his curtains.

"What are you doing?" she asked.

"Going home," answered the goblin. "You don't suppose I'm going to stay here with a nasty old woman who tells stories, do you? We Very-Little-Goblins hate that!"

"Oh, don't go," begged Mrs Biscuit. "Don't go! Everyone will wonder why you've gone."

"Oh no, they won't, because I shall tell them," said the goblin, tying up his carpet into a roll.

"Please, please, Goblin, stay with me. I'll make you a beautiful little garden seat out of chocolate and ginger if you'll stay," begged Mrs Biscuit. "And I won't tell stories any more, I promise."

"Well, if you do, I'll tell people the truth," said the goblin, unrolling his carpet again. "So you be careful, Mrs Biscuit."

Mrs Biscuit was very careful for a few days and the goblin didn't speak a word. Then one morning, a poor beggar-woman came in and asked Mrs Biscuit for a stale cake.

"A stale cake? Why, I haven't such a thing in the place!" cried Mrs Biscuit. "Be off with you!"

"Oh, you mean old woman!" cried the goblin's tiny voice, and he flung open his chocolate front door. "Where are those cakes you baked last Thursday that haven't been sold yet?"

"I've eaten them myself," said Mrs Biscuit in a rage. "Mind your own business!"

"You're a storyteller," said the goblin. "There they are up on that shelf. You give them to the poor beggar-woman this very minute, or I'll go back to Mushroom Town."

Mrs Biscuit dragged the cakes down, put them into a bag and threw them across the counter. The beggar-woman thanked her and went off with them.

Mrs Biscuit didn't care to say anything to the goblin, but she was very angry. He went into his sugar house and slammed the door. He was angry too, to think that anyone could be so mean.

That afternoon a thin little boy crept

into the shop and asked for a stale crust. He was dreadfully hungry, and Mrs Biscuit stared at him crossly. Another beggar!

She was just going to say that she had no stale crusts when she saw the goblin peeping at her out of one of the windows of his sugar house. She hurriedly took down half a stale loaf and gave it to the little boy.

He was so grateful that he took her plump hand and kissed it. It was the first time that Mrs Biscuit had been kissed for years, and dear me, she did like it! She suddenly smiled at the little boy, and felt sorry to see how thin he was. And then she took down a fine new chocolate cake, and gave it to him.

"Oh!" he said in delight. "You kind woman! Is that really for me?"

He went out of the shop singing. Mrs Biscuit looked at the place on her hand where the little boy had kissed it, and a nice warm feeling crept into her heart. It was really rather pleasant to be kind, she thought. She would try it again.

She looked up and saw a crowd of
people looking in at her window. And she
saw that the goblin was doing a strange,
light-hearted little dance round and
round the top of the cake, making all the
passers-by stare in surprise.

"What are you doing that for?" she
asked in astonishment.

"Oh, I'm so pleased to see you do a
kind act that I've got to dance!" said the
tiny goblin. Everyone watched him, and

soon quite a dozen people came in to buy cakes. Mrs Biscuit did a good morning's trade.

The next time someone came begging, Mrs Biscuit decided to be kind and generous again, to get the nice warm feeling in her heart. So she packed up a cherry pie in a box and put some ginger buns in a bag for the old man who came asking for a crust. He was so surprised and delighted that he could hardly say thank you. The little goblin threw open his door and began to sing a loud song all about Mrs Biscuit's kindness, and soon half the village came to hear it. Mrs Biscuit blushed red, and didn't know where to look.

Then Mr Straw, the farmer, came to buy a big ginger cake for his wife's birthday. Now, there were two ginger cakes in the shop, one baked a good time back and one baked that very morning. Mrs Biscuit took up the stale one and popped it into a bag.

"You're sure that's fresh, now?" said Farmer Straw. Mrs Biscuit opened her

mouth to say untruthfully that it was, when she stopped.

No, that would be a mean, unkind thing to say, especially when the cake was for Mrs Straw's birthday.

"Er – well, no, this one isn't very fresh," she said. "I'll give you a fresher one, only baked this morning."

The little goblin, who was peeping out of his window, ready to cry out that she was a storyteller, gave a shout of delight.

"She's a truthful old dame!" he cried. "She's a kind old woman!"

"Dear me," said Farmer Straw, looking round. "That's your little goblin, isn't it? Well, it's nice of you to let me have the fresh cake, Mrs Biscuit, when you've got one that is not quite so fresh. I'm much obliged to you. Perhaps you'll be good enough to come to my wife's birthday party this afternoon?"

"I'd be very pleased to," said Mrs Biscuit, thankful that she hadn't given him the stale cake – for how dreadful it would have been to go to a birthday party and see everyone eating a stale cake she had sold as fresh?

Well, that was the last time Mrs Biscuit ever thought of telling a story or being mean. She felt so nice when she had told the truth or been kind to someone that she soon found she simply couldn't tell a story or be unkind any more. And in a short time people liked her so much that they always bought their cakes and pies from her, and she became rich enough to buy a little cottage and go there to live.

She took the iced cake with her, with the little sugar house on top. She put it on a table in the front window to remind her of the days when she had kept a cake shop – and would you believe it? – that

Very-Little-Goblin is still there, shaking his carpet every day and opening his windows to let in the sunshine!

That shows she is still a truthful, kind old dame, and if you ever pass her cottage and see the iced cake in the window, with the little sugar house on top, don't be afraid of knocking at her door and asking if you may see the Very-Little-Goblin. Mrs Biscuit will be delighted to show you round.

The Boy Who Wouldn't go to Bed

Timothy was such a naughty boy at bedtime. He never wanted to go to bed, and when his mother said, "Put your toys away now, Timmy," he always began to cry and stamp his feet.

"I don't want to go to bed!" he shouted. "Why must I go? Why can't I stay up all night? I'm not sleepy. Let me stay up!"

And Mother always said, "No, Timmy dear, you can't stay up. Little boys must go to bed early. Nobody stays up all night."

One night Timmy was so very naughty about going to bed that his mother really didn't know what to do with him. You should have heard how bad he was! He kicked all his bricks round the nursery, he stamped on his best soldier, he shouted at his mother, and tried to slap her when she made him pick up his toys. In the middle of it all, in came Timothy's father to see what was the matter. When he heard Mother's story, he looked very serious.

"Very well, Timmy," he said, "you shall do what you want. We won't bother with you any more this evening. You shall stay up all night if you want to."

Stay up all night! Timmy could hardly believe his ears! Good! He had got his own way at last. His parents went out of the room and shut the door. Timmy was left alone in the playroom and his parents went downstairs.

He had a lovely time until eight o'clock, building an enormous tower with his bricks. Then until nine o'clock he drew in his drawing-book. The last thing he drew was a giant with four eyes, and he was very pleased with that. But when he shut up his book, he didn't feel quite so pleased. Everything seemed so quiet and still. Surely his parents hadn't gone to bed yet! Why, it was only nine o'clock! Suppose that a giant came into the playroom at night! It wouldn't be very nice, and he might be surprised to see Timmy sitting up so late.

"There aren't any giants nowadays," said Timmy to himself. "What shall I do now? I'll get my book and read."

He got out his big book of animals and began to read it. He liked it very much until he came to a picture of a lion

roaring. A noise in the street, outside the window, suddenly made him jump.

"I quite thought it was a lion for a moment," said Timmy, shutting up his book. "It's ten o'clock – I'll get out my big puzzle and do it on the rug."

He took his box of jigsaw puzzles from the toy cupboard and emptied the bits on to the rug. Timmy felt rather cold, so he sat as near the radiator as he could.

It took a long time to do the puzzle, and just as he was finishing it he heard footsteps going up the stairs.

"That's Jane going to bed," he said. "I wonder if Mummy and Daddy have gone too."

Just then the door opened and Jane, his big sister, looked in.

"Well, Timmy, I'm off to bed," she said. "Do you want to come too, like a sensible little boy, or shall I leave you here all alone?"

"I'm not going to bed tonight, Jane," said Timothy. "Mummy said I could stay

up all night, and I'm going to."

"Oh, very well," said Jane, and she closed the door and went into her bedroom. Timmy heard her running the water in the bathroom, and then heard the creak of her bed as she got into it. He opened the playroom door and looked out. Everything was dark. There wasn't a light on anywhere.

"The house will soon be asleep too," said Timmy. "I shall be the only one awake!"

He went back to the radiator, which was getting cold now, and sat down to his puzzle again. He put a few pieces of the puzzle into their places, and then suddenly he yawned. His eyes felt as if they had sand in them, and he rubbed them hard. He wasn't going to go to sleep, not he! He was going to stay up all night!

He didn't want to do any more puzzles. He put all the pieces away, and then sat down in his little chair. How quiet the house was! There wasn't a sound to be heard.

Crack! What was that? Timmy sat up straight and listened. *Crack!* There was the noise again. Why, it was the big toy-cupboard making that noise. It sometimes did it in the daytime, but it didn't sound so loud then. It sounded very loud indeed at night.

Then the old wicker-chair in the corner creaked all by itself, and Timmy was very much surprised. Could somebody be sitting down in it? And whatever could that be, scampering over the floor? Ooh, he didn't like it!

Poor Timmy! It was only a little mouse come out to pick up the crumbs on the floor. When it saw Timmy it was frightened – but not nearly so frightened as Timmy was! He didn't know it was only a mouse. He couldn't think what it was!

Then the wind began to blow outside, and it puffed round the window and said "Hoo-hoo-hoo," in a very loud voice. How Timmy jumped with fright!

"Hoo-hoo-hoo," said the wind. "HOO-HOO-HOO!"

"I wish I was in bed," thought Timmy, "I wish I was cuddled down fast asleep under my warm blankets. It's cold in here, and I'm sleepy and frightened – but I daren't go to sleep in case the wind comes right in through the window and shouts in my ear."

He sat curled up in his chair and listened to the wind blowing. A twig tapped on the window and he didn't like that at all. And then suddenly he heard the front door being opened!

"Burglars!" thought poor Timmy, and he was so frightened that he couldn't move a finger.

But it wasn't burglars! It was his mother and father coming home late from a party. They hadn't gone to bed, they had been out all the evening!

Mother ran upstairs to see if Timmy was still up, and when she opened the playroom door, what a sleepy, frightened little boy she saw! He was curled up in his chair, quite sure that it was a burglar coming upstairs, and dear me, how glad he was to see his mother!

He ran to her and hugged her as if he would never let her go.

"Oh, I'm so glad it's you!" he said.

"I thought I'd just pop in and see how you felt," said Mother. "Daddy and I are going to bed now, but you want to stay up all night, don't you?"

"Oh no, please, no," said Timmy. "I want to go to bed. I don't like staying up late. Put me to bed, Mummy, please."

"But I thought you didn't like going to bed," said his mother. "Oh, I think

you must stay up all night, Timmy dear.
You said you wanted to, you know."

"Well, I don't want to now," said
Timmy. "Let me go to bed, Mummy. I
promise I'll never, never be naughty
about going to bed again, if only you'll
put me to bed now."

"Very well," said his mother. "I'll put
you to bed – but mind, Timmy, if ever I
have any more naughtiness at bedtime,
you will certainly stay up all night – and
you won't like that at all, will you?"

"No, I shan't," said Timmy, and goodness me, you should have seen how quickly he got undressed! His mother popped him into bed, and in two shakes of a lamb's tail he was fast asleep.

And at seven o'clock the next night, when his mother said, "Put your toys away, Timmy, it's bedtime!" you should have seen him hurry. He wasn't going to miss his bedtime again! No, he was definitely going to bed!

You Bad
Little Dog

John and Fiona took their little dog Wuff
down to the sands with them. It was such
a lovely beach for little dogs, as well as for
children!

There was fine golden sand stretching
right down to the very edge of the sea
and tiny waves to play in, and warm
pools to bathe in. Wuff liked it as much as
John and Fiona did.

That morning the children had their
spades with them. They meant to build
the biggest castle on the beach – bigger
even than Tom and Peter and Dick had
built the week before. That one was so
big that the sea just couldn't knock it all
down, but left half of it for the next day.

Wuff wanted to build, too – but as his
idea of building was to dig enormous

95

holes and scatter the sand all over the place, John and Fiona wouldn't let him help.

"No," they said. "You keep away today, Wuff. You're just being a nuisance. As soon as we get a heap built up you scrape a hole in it. That's not building!"

So Wuff went a little way away and sat down sadly to look at the two children building. Soon an old man came and sat down in a deckchair nearby. He opened his newspaper and began to read. He wasn't near the children, and they took no notice of him at all.

But Wuff was quite near him, sitting still, feeling rather bored. He suddenly smelled rather a nice smell. He got up and ambled round and about, sniffing at the sand. Ah – here was the smell!

Someone had left a bit of cake in the sand and Wuff felt that he really must dig it up. So he began to scrape violently with his front paws. Up into the air went great showers of fine sand – and the old man found himself being covered from head to foot.

"Stop it," he growled to Wuff. But Wuff was too happy to hear. He was getting near that bit of cake! Up flew some more sand, and down it came on the old man's newspaper, making a little rattling noise.

The man jumped up in anger. He picked up some seaweed and threw it at Wuff. "Bad dog, you! Go away! They shouldn't allow dogs on the beach. I've always said so! Grrrrr!"

The seaweed hit Wuff and he yelped and ran off. He was frightened, too, when the man made the growling noise because it sounded like a big dog!

The children were very cross when they saw the old man throwing seaweed at Wuff and heard him shouting. "Just because Wuff threw some sand over him by mistake!" said Fiona.

"You take that nasty little dog of yours away from this beach!" shouted the old man. "If he comes near me again he'll be sorry!"

Fiona and John were upset. They left their castle half-finished, and Wuff left the hidden bit of cake, and they all went right to the other end of the beach. They began to build another castle, but it was lunch-time before they had done very much. They were very disappointed.

"Now the sea will be able to sweep away all we've done," said John. "The castle ought to be twice as high if there's to be any left when the tide goes out again."

They went home to lunch, Wuff dancing round their legs. The old man had gone, too. The deckchair was empty and the deckchair-man was just about to pile it with all the others, so that the sea wouldn't take it away when the tide came in.

Next morning the children went down to the beach again. Wuff went, too. The old man was there in his chair, and John and Fiona decided not to go too near him.

"We really must work hard this morning," said John. "Granny is coming this afternoon and it would be lovely to show her a really magnificent castle, bigger than any on the beach."

"Wuff," said Wuff, quite agreeing.

"You go away till we've finished," said Fiona to Wuff. "Look, take your ball and go over there to play with it. You aren't much good at castles, Wuff."

Wuff took his ball. But it was really very boring to play by himself, and he suddenly remembered the bit of cake he had smelled in the sand the day before. Suppose it was still there? He could perhaps find it this time. He began to run about, sniffing, to see if he could smell it again.

He came near to the old man and

stopped. Why, here was the man who growled like a dog and threw seaweed at him! He'd better be careful or he might be hit by another piece of soggy seaweed.

The old man sat quite still. He didn't speak or move. Wuff sniffed the air. Was he asleep? When people were asleep they didn't shout or throw things. He could look for that bit of cake if the old man was asleep.

He *was* asleep – fast asleep in the warm sun. His newspaper lay on his knee. The wind tugged at it, trying to get it.

Wuff began to scrape in the sand for the bit of cake. A few grains flew into the air and fell on the newspaper on the man's knee. He didn't stir at all. The wind suddenly blew strongly and the newspaper flapped hard. It flapped itself right off the man's knee on to the sand.

Wuff stopped burrowing and looked at it. Soon that newspaper would blow right away. He didn't know why people liked newspapers so much, but he knew they did. This one belonged to the old man. Did he want it? Would he mind if his paper blew right into the sea?

The children suddenly saw Wuff near the old man again. They called to him. "Wuff! Wuff! Come away from there! You know you got into trouble yesterday."

Then John saw the newspaper blowing away. "Look," he said, "the paper has blown off that man's knee. He must be asleep. There it goes! Oh, won't he be cross when he wakes up and finds that the sea has got it!"

"It will serve him right for throwing seaweed at Wuff," said Fiona.

"There goes the paper – almost into that pool," said John. "Wuff – fetch it, then, fetch it, boy!"

Wuff raced after the paper and pounced on it just before it flew into the pool! The old man, awakened by the shouting, sat up and looked round to see what the noise was about.

He saw Wuff pouncing on his paper – and then the little black dog turned and ran all the way back to the old man with it and put it down by his feet, just as he did when he ran after a ball and took it back to the children.

"Why, you good, clever dog!" said the old man, patting him. "Good dog, good boy! Who do you belong to?"

"He belongs to us," said John and Fiona, coming up, astonished to find the man making such a fuss of Wuff.

"Well, he's a very clever dog," said the man, folding up his newspaper. "Not a bit like a horrid little dog I saw here yesterday, who threw sand all over me. Oh, he was a dreadful little thing!"

"Wuff!" said Wuff, trying to tell the man that yesterday's dog and today's were exactly the same. But the man didn't understand.

"I must buy a bone for this good dog," said the man. "Does he like bones?"

"Yes. But he likes ice creams even better," said Fiona.

"Well, well – what good taste he has!" said the man, getting up. "Shall we all go and buy ice creams? Come along, then."

They went to the ice cream man and the old man bought four ice creams, one for each of them and one for Wuff too, of course. Then he went down to look at the castle the children were building.

"I'd better help you with this," he said. "I can see you won't finish it if I don't.

105

We'll make it the biggest one ever seen!"

They finished their ice creams, Wuff too, and set to work. My goodness me, how the old man could dig! You should have seen that castle when it was finished. All the children on the beach came to admire it.

"Well, thank you very much indeed for the ice creams and the digging," said John and Fiona.

"I'll help you again tomorrow," said the man, smiling. "Goodbye – and goodbye, little dog. I'm glad you're not like the nasty little dog I shouted at yesterday!"

Off he went. The two children looked at one another. "Well! He may think Wuff is a different dog – but honestly he's a different man, too!" said John. "Who would have guessed he could be so nice?"

It was funny, wasn't it? What a good thing Wuff ran after his paper!

The Enchanted Egg

Now once upon a time Sly-One the gnome did a marvellous piece of magic that nobody had ever done before.

He stirred together in a golden bowl, lit by moonlight, many peculiar things. One of them was the breath of a bat, another was a snippet of lightning, and yet another was an echo he had got from a deep cave.

He didn't quite know what would come of all these strange things and the dozens of others he had mixed together – but he guessed it would be something very powerful indeed.

"Whatever it is, it will bring me greatness and power," thought Sly-One, stirring hard. "I shall be able to do what I like."

Sly-One was not a nice person. He was mean and unkind and sly. Nobody liked him, though most people were afraid of him because he was very cunning. But he did not use his brains for good things, only for bad ones.

He stirred away for two whole hours, and soon the curious mixture in the golden bowl began to turn a colour that Sly-One had never in his life seen before. Then it began to boil! As it boiled, it twittered!

"Very strange indeed," said Sly-One to himself, half scared. "A very curious twitter indeed. It sounds like the twitter of the magic hoolloopolony bird, which hasn't been seen for five hundred years. Surely this magic mixture of mine isn't going to make a hoolloopolony bird! How I wish it was, because if I had that bird I could do anything I liked. It is so magic that it has the power to obey every order I give it. Why, I could be king of the whole world in a day!"

But the mixture didn't make a bird. It twittered for a little while longer, turned another curious colour, and then boiled away to nothing.

Or almost nothing. When Sly-One, disappointed, looked into the bowl, he saw something small lying at the bottom of it. It was a tiny yellow egg, with a red spot at each end.

Sly-One got very excited indeed when he saw it. "It's not a hoolloopolony bird – but it's the egg! My word, it's a hoolloopolony's egg! Now, if only I can

get it hatched, I shall have one of those enchanted birds for my very own – a slave that can obey any order I think of making!"

He picked up the egg very gently. It hummed in his fingers and he put it back into the bowl. How was he to get it hatched?

"I'd better find a bird's nest and put it there," thought Sly-One. "A really fine nest, safe and warm and cosy, where this enchanted egg can rest and be hatched out. I must go round and inspect all the nests there are. I shall soon find a good one."

He left the egg in the bowl and covered it with a silver sheet. Then he put on his boots and went out. It was the nesting season for birds, and Sly-One knew there would be plenty of nests to choose from.

He soon found one. It was a robin's, built in a ditch. Sly-One walked up to inspect it, and kneeled down beside it.

"It's made of moss and dead leaves and bits of grass," he said. "It's well-hidden because there are plenty of dead

leaves lying all round. Perhaps this will do."

But just then a dog came sniffing into the ditch and Sly-One changed his mind. "No, no! It's not a good place for a nest, if dogs can tramp about near it. Why, that dog might easily put his paw on the enchanted egg and smash it, if I put it here!"

So he went off to find another nest. He saw some big ones high up in a tree and he went up to look at them. They were rooks' nests, big and roomy.

"They look safe enough, high up here," thought Sly-One. "Made of good strong twigs too. No dog could tread on these high nests!"

He sat down in one to see what it was like. Just then a big wind blew and the tree rocked the nest violently. Sly-One was frightened. He climbed out quickly.

"Good gracious!" he said to the rooks. "I wonder you build your nests quite so high in the trees. The wind will blow your nests to and fro and out will come your eggs!"

"Caw!" said a big rook, scornfully. "Don't you know that when a stormy summer is expected we build lower down

and when a calm one comes, we build high up? We always know! No wind will blow our nests down. Why do you come to visit them, Sly-One? You don't lay eggs!"

Sly-One didn't answer. He slid down the tree and came to a hole in the trunk. He put his head in and saw a heap of sawdust at the bottom. It was a little owl's nest. Sly-One felt about, and didn't like it.

"Not at all comfortable for an enchanted egg," he thought. "A good idea though for a nest, deep down in a tree-hole. Very, very safe!"

"If you want another kind of hole, ask the kingfisher to show you his," hissed the little owl. "Do you want to hide from your enemies or something, Sly-One? Then the kingfisher's nest is just the place!"

So Sly-One went to the brilliant kingfisher who sat on a low branch over the river and watched for fish. "Where is your nest?" asked Sly-One.

"Down there, in that hole in the bank,"

said the kingfisher, pointing with his big, strong beak. "Right at the end. You'll see it easily."

Sly-One found the hole and crawled into it. At the end was a peculiar nest, made of old fish-bones arranged together. It smelled horrible.

"I feel sick!" said Sly-One, and crawled out quickly. "Fancy making a nest of smelly old fish-bones! Certainly I shan't put my precious enchanted egg there!"

He saw the house martins flying in the air above him and he called to them. "Where are your nests? I want to find a nice, cosy, safe one to put something precious in."

"See that house?" said a house martin, flying close to him. "See the eaves there? Well, just underneath we have built our nests. They are made of mud, Sly-One."

"What!" said Sly-One, looking up at the curious mud-nests in amazement. "Are those your nests – those peculiar things made of mud, stuck against the walls of the house? They might fall down at any minute! And fancy living in a mud-nest! No, that won't do, thank you."

"Coo-ooo," said a woodpigeon, flying near. "Would my nest do for you, Sly-One? I don't know what you want it for – but I have a very nice nest indeed."

"What's it made of?" asked Sly-One.

"Oh – just two sticks and a little bit of

moss!" said the woodpigeon, and showed Sly-One the tree in which she had built her nest.

"Why, you can see right through it, it's so flimsy!" said Sly-One in horror, thinking that his enchanted egg would certainly fall through the pigeon's nest, and land on the ground below.

Then he went to the lark, but the lark said that she just laid her eggs in a dent in the ground. She showed him her eggs, laid in a horse's hoofmark in a field.

"Ridiculous!" said Sly-One. "Why, anyone might run over those eggs and smash them. A most stupid place for a nest. I want somewhere that nobody could possibly tread in."

"Well," said the lark, offended, "why not go up to the steep cliffs, then, where some of the sea-birds lay their eggs. Look, do you see the great bird there? He's a guillemot. Call him down and ask him to carry you to where he puts his eggs. They are up on the steep cliffs, where nobody can even climb."

Soon Sly-One was being carried on the

guillemot's strong wings to the high cliff. There, on a ledge, was a big egg, laid by the guillemot.

"Do you mean to say you just put it there on this ledge?" said Sly-One. "It might fall off at any moment, when the wind blows strongly."

"Oh no it won't," said the guillemot. "Do you see its strange shape? It's made that way, narrow at one end, so that when the wind blows, it just rolls round and round in the same place. It doesn't fall off."

"Oh," said Sly-One. He thought of his enchanted egg. No, that wasn't the right shape to roll round and round. It would certainly roll right off the cliff if the wind blew. It wouldn't be any good putting it there and asking the guillemot to hatch it for him.

He went to see a few nests made of seaweed, that other sea-birds showed him. But they smelled too strong, and he didn't like them. He went back to the wood near his home, wondering and wondering what nest would be best for his precious egg.

He saw a long-tailed tit go to her nest in a bush. He parted the branches and looked at it. It was a most extraordinary ball-shaped little nest, made of hundreds and hundreds of soft feathers! Perhaps it would be just right for the hoolloopolony egg.

"There's no room for another egg," said the long-tailed tit. "I have to bend my long tail right over my head as it is,

118

when I sit in my ball of a nest. When my eleven eggs hatch out, there won't be any room at all!"

Then Sly-One met a big grey bird, with a barred chest. The bird called "Cuckoo!" to him and made him jump.

"Oh, cuckoo, so you're back again," said Sly-One. "Where's your nest?"

"I don't make one," said the cuckoo. "I always choose a good, cosy, safe nest to put my eggs in, belonging to somebody else. I don't bother about building!"

"Well," said Sly-One, "as you're used to finding good nests for your eggs, perhaps you can help me. I want one for an enchanted egg. I want a good safe nest,

with a bird who will hatch out my egg and look after the baby bird for me, till it's old enough to come to me and do magic spells."

"Ah, I'm the one to help you then," said the cuckoo at once. "I can pick up eggs in my beak easily. I've just put an egg into a wagtail's nest. Wagtails make good parents. I'll put your enchanted egg there too, if you like."

And that's just what the cuckoo did. Sly-One fetched the little egg from the golden bowl, and the cuckoo took it in her beak and popped it into the wagtail's nest up in the ivy. She showed Sly-One her own egg there too.

"The wagtail had four eggs of her own," she said. "I took one out and dropped it on the ground when I put my own there. I've taken a second one out now to make way for your enchanted egg. The wagtail will sit on all four eggs and keep them warm, mine, yours, and two of her own."

Sly-One was pleased. "Now my egg will be safe," he thought. "How clever the cuckoo is! She's used to finding good nests for her eggs. I ought to have asked her advice at first, instead of wasting my time inspecting all those other nests."

One day Sly-One went to see how his egg was getting on, and to his surprise the cuckoo's egg had already hatched, though it had been laid after the wagtail's eggs. And also to his surprise, there was only one wagtail egg in the nest, besides his own enchanted egg. Sly-One saw the other one lying broken on the ground. He wondered what had happened.

He didn't know the habits of the baby

cuckoo. That little bare, black, baby bird didn't like anything in the nest with him. He had actually pitched the wagtail's egg out of the nest! Now he was lying resting, waiting for strength to pitch the other eggs out too!

He did pitch out one egg – the other wagtail egg. He waited till the mother wagtail was off the nest for a few minutes, then he set to work. He got the wagtail egg into a little hollow on his back, climbed slowly up the side of the nest – and then over went the little egg to the ground below. Another egg gone. Now there was only the hoolloopolony egg left to deal with. The baby cuckoo sank back, exhausted.

Then the enchanted egg hatched out into a dainty little yellow bird with a red head. It lay in the nest close to the baby cuckoo. When the wagtail came back she looked at the two baby birds and loved them. She didn't know they were not really her own.

"I'll go and fetch grubs for you," she said, and flew off.

As soon as she was gone the baby cuckoo wanted to have the nest all to himself. What was this warm bundle pressing close against him? He didn't like it. In fact he couldn't bear it!

Somehow he managed to get the tiny bird on to his back. Somehow he managed to climb up the side of the nest to the top. He gave a heave – and over the top of the nest went the baby hoolloopolony bird, right to the ground below.

It twittered there helplessly. The wag-tail came back but didn't notice it. She fed the hungry baby cuckoo and thought what a wonderful child he was. She didn't seem to miss the other at all.

When Sly-One came along to see how his wonderful egg was getting on, he found only the baby cuckoo there in the nest! On the ground lay the tiny hoolloopolony bird, almost dead.

Sly-One gave a cry. He picked up the tiny bird and put it into his pocket to keep it warm. He sped to the wise woman

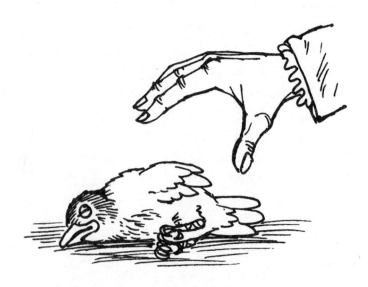

with it, and begged her to keep it alive.

"Sly-One," said the wise woman. "I know why you want this bird. When it grows, it will be able to do powerful magic for you. Well, Sly-One, you are not a nice person and I am not going to rear up a bird to work for you. It must die!"

Sly-One was very angry. "How was I to know the bad ways of baby cuckoos?" he cried. "The cuckoo is not a good bird. It puts its eggs into other birds' nests and throws out their own eggs. And the baby cuckoo throws them out too, and even throws out the baby birds. They are both bad – but how was I to know?"

"You are not really very clever, Sly-One," said the wise woman, softly. "I could have told you the ways of all birds and animals, though you should know them yourself. I am glad you chose the cuckoo to help you! Now you will never own a hoolloopolony bird, and you will never be king of the world!"

He wasn't of course, and a very good thing too. As for the tiny bird, it did live, though Sly-One didn't know. The wise woman kept it alive, and then set it free. It is full of magic, but no one knows that. It's no good trying to catch it if you see it, because it can't be caught.

Whose nest would you have put the egg into? There are such a lot of different ones to choose from, aren't there?

Silly Simon and the Goat

Simon had had a cold and his ears had ached. He had been very miserable. Now he was better and up again, but he was rather deaf. That was horrid.

"You'll be able to go to school again tomorrow," said his mother. "That will be nice for you. Today you can stay at home and help me."

So Simon helped his mother. He fetched in the washing from the line. He ran to the shop to get some butter, and he took the baby out for a little walk. He really was a great help.

"You have been quite a sensible boy for once," said his mother, pleased. Silly Simon wasn't always sensible. He sometimes did very silly things, and then his mother was cross.

He was pleased. "Well, you always think I haven't got brains," he said. "But I have, Mum. I'm really a very clever boy."

"Well, I hope you go on being a clever boy for the rest of the day," said his mother. "Now, I'm going upstairs to do some things. Baby is fast asleep."

She went upstairs, and then she remembered that she wanted her old coat to mend. So she called down to Simon.

"Simon! Fetch me the old coat, will you?"

Simon didn't hear her very well. He thought his mother said, "Fetch me the old goat." He was rather surprised, but still, as he was feeling very good and obedient, he set off to fetch the old goat in from the field.

He caught the goat, and led him to the house on a rope. He called up to his mother. "I've got it for you."

"Well, bring it upstairs, and hang it over the banisters," called his mother. Simon felt more astonished than before.

It was funny to want the old goat
brought into the house, but still stranger
to want it upstairs hung over the
banisters.

"The goat won't like it!" he called up
after a bit. But his mother only half-
heard what he said.

"Don't be silly!" she said. "It won't
hurt the coat. But hang it in the hall, if
you'd rather."

"Hang you in the hall?" said Simon to the surprised goat. "Which would you rather, goat? I can hang you in the hall, or take you upstairs and put you over the banisters."

The goat didn't seem to mind which. So Simon took it into the hall and looked at the pegs there. He tried to tie the rope to a peg, but the goat broke away at once, pulling the peg-rack down with a crash.

"Simon!" shouted his mother crossly. "What in the world are you doing? Be quiet."

"There!" said Simon to the goat. "You'll be getting into trouble if you make noises like that. You'd better come upstairs. I think it would be easier to put you over the banisters, after all."

So the goat was dragged upstairs. It made a great noise and Simon's mother called out again.

"You'll wake the baby! What are you making all that noise for?"

"I'm dragging the goat up," panted Simon. "It won't come."

"A coat isn't as heavy as all that," said

his mother, crossly. "What a fuss you make to be sure! I hope you're not dragging it on the floor."

Simon at last got the goat to the top of the stairs. He tried to get it across the banisters, but the goat simply wouldn't go. As fast as Simon lifted it up one end, it slipped to the ground the other end. It was a most annoying goat.

"Simon! Whatever are you doing out there?" called his mother. "Why can't you be quiet?"

"There!" said Simon to the goat fiercely. "You'll get me into trouble if you don't behave. Now, just you let me put you across the banisters!"

But it was no good. The goat wouldn't be at all helpful. It clattered with its four feet, it slid here and there, and was altogether most obstinate.

It suddenly got very tired of Simon. It backed a little way, put its head down, ran at Simon and caught him full on its head. It butted him hard, and Simon rose in the air with a yell, sailed down the stairs, and landed at the bottom with a

crash. He howled loudly. The baby woke up and yelled, too.

Simon's mother flung open the door to glare at Simon – but instead she found herself glaring at the old goat, who glared back, and looked as if he might butt her at any moment. Simon's mother hurriedly stepped back into the room and shut the door.

She called through it. "You bad boy, Simon! How dare you bring that old goat up here? Take him back to the field at once!"

"Well, you told me to bring him here and hang him over the banisters," wailed Simon. "You did, you did!"

"Oh! Oh, you foolish, silly, stupid boy!" cried his mother. "I told you to fetch my old coat – I wanted to mend it! Oh, why did I ever say you were good and sensible today?"

The goat trotted neatly downstairs and into the hall. It went into the kitchen and out of the back door. It had had enough of Simon and Simon's mother and the crying baby.

"It's gone!" said Simon. "But, oh, Mum, it's taken a rug with it to eat!"

"Oh, has it!" cried his mother, and shot out of the room and downstairs to catch the goat. But she was too late. The goat had eaten the rug.

Then Simon got sent up to his room, and he was very upset about it.

"I try to be good and sensible and

obedient and this is what I get for it!" he wept. "I'll never try again."

"Well, if you do things like that when you are trying to be good, you'd better stop!" said his mother.

Poor Simon! You wouldn't think anyone would be so silly, would you?

The
Witch's Cat

Old Dame Kirri was a witch. You could tell she was because she had bright green eyes. She was a good witch though, and spent most of her time making good spells to help people who were ill or unhappy.

She lived in Toppling Cottage, which was just like its name and looked exactly as if it was going to topple over. But it was kept up by strong magic and not a brick had fallen, although the cottage was five hundred years old.

At the back of the cottage was the witch's garden. Round it ran a very, very high wall, taller than the tallest man.

"I like a high wall. It keeps people from peeping and prying," said old witch Kirri. "In my garden I grow a lot of strange and powerful herbs. I don't want people

136

to see them and steal them. I won't have people making spells from my magic herbs – they might make bad ones."

The witch had a cat. It was black and big, and had green eyes very like the witch's. Its name was Cinder-Boy.

Cinder-Boy helped the witch with her spells. He was really a remarkably clever cat. He knew how to sit exactly in the middle of a chalk ring without moving, while Kirri the witch danced round and sang spells. He knew how to go out and collect dewdrops in the moonlight. He took a special little silver cup for that, and never spilled a drop.

He never drank milk. He liked tea, made as strong as the witch made for herself. Sometimes he would sit and sip his tea and purr, and the witch would sip her tea and purr, too. It was funny to see them.

Cinder-Boy loved to sleep in the walled-in garden. He knew all the flowers and herbs which grew there. No weeds were allowed to grow. Cinder-Boy scratched them all up.

But one day he came to a small plant growing at the foot of the wall. It had leaves like a rose-tree. It had pale pink flowers, with a mass of yellow stamens in the middle. It smelled very sweet.

"What flower are you?" said Cinder-Boy. "You smell rather like a rose."

"Well, that's just what I am," said the plant. "I'm a wild rose."

"How did you get here?" said Cinder-Boy, surprised.

"A bird dropped a seed," said the wild rose. "But I don't like being here, black cat."

"My name is Cinder-Boy," said the

138

witch's cat. "Why don't you like being here? It is a very nice place to be."

"Well, I feel shut in," said the wild rose. "I'm not very large. If I was taller than the wall I could grow up into the air, and see over the top. I don't like being down here at the bottom, shut in."

"Well, grow tall then," said Cinder-Boy. "I can give you a spell to make your stems nice and long, if you like. Then you can reach up to the top of the wall and look over. There's a nice view there, I can tell you."

"Oh, would you do that?" said the wild rose in delight. "Thank you!"

So Cinder-Boy went off to get a spell which would make the stems of the wild rose grow very long. He soon found one. It was in a small blue bottle, and he poured it into a watering-can. The spell was blue, too.

Then he watered the wild rose with the spell, and it began to work almost at once. In two or three days the stems of

the wild rose plant had grown quite high into the air.

"Go on growing. You will soon be at the top of the wall!" said Cinder-Boy. So the wild rose went on, making its stems longer and longer, hoping to get to the very top of the wall.

But when Cinder-Boy next strolled out into the garden to see how it was getting on, what a shock he had! Every single stem was bent over and lay sprawling over the grass!

"Why, what has happened?" said Cinder-Boy, waving his tail in surprise.

"My stalks grew tall, but they didn't grow strong," said the wild rose, sadly. "Just as I reached the top of the wall, they all flopped over and fell down. They are not strong enough to bear their own weight."

"Well, how do plants with weak stems manage to climb high then?" said Cinder-Boy, puzzled. "Runner beans grow high and they have very weak stems. Sweet-peas grow high, and they have weak stems too. I'll go and see how they do it." So off he went, for the witch grew both in the garden. He soon came back.

"The beans twine their stalks round poles," he said, "and the sweetpeas grow little green fingers, called tendrils, which catch hold of things, and they pull themselves up high like that. Can't you do that?"

The wild rose couldn't. It didn't know how to. Its stems wouldn't twist themselves, however much it tried to make them do so. And it couldn't grow a tendril at all.

"Well, we must think of another way," said the cat.

"Cinder-Boy, how do you get up to the top of the wall?" asked the wild rose. "You are often up there in the sun. I see you. Well, how do you get to the top?"

"I run up the trees," said Cinder-Boy. "Do you see the young fruit-trees near you? Well, I run up those to the top of the wall. I use my claws to help me. I dig them into the bark of the trees, and hold on with them."

He showed the wild rose his big curved

142

claws. "I can put them in or out as I like," he said. "They are very useful claws."

The wild rose thought they were too. "If I grew claws like that I could easily climb up the fruit-trees, right through them to the top, and then I'd be waving at the top of the wall," it said. "Can't you get me some claws like yours, Cinder-Boy?"

The cat blinked his green eyes and thought hard. "I know what I could do," he said. "I could ask the witch Kirri, my mistress, to make some magic claws that would grow on you. I'll ask her today. In return you must promise to grow her some lovely scarlet rosehips which she can trim her hats and bonnets with in the autumn."

"Oh, I will, I will," promised the wild rose. So Cinder-Boy went off to the witch Kirri and asked her for what he wanted.

She grumbled a little. "It is difficult to make claws," she said. "Very difficult. You will have to help me, Cinder-Boy. You will have to sit in the middle of a blue ring of chalk, and put out all your claws at once, while I sing a magic song. Don't be scared at what happens."

In the middle of the garden the witch drew a chalk ring and Cinder-Boy went to sit in the middle of it. He stuck out all his claws as she commanded and she danced round with her broomstick singing such a magic song that Cinder-Boy felt quite scared. Then a funny thing happened.

His claws fell out on to the ground with a clatter – and they turned red or

green as they fell. He looked at his paws and saw new ones growing. Then those fell out, too. How very, very strange!

Soon there was quite a pile of claws on the ground. Then the witch stopped singing and dancing, and rubbed out the ring of chalk.

"You can come out now, Cinder-Boy," she said. "The magic is finished."

Cinder-Boy collected all the red and green claws. They were strong and curved and sharp. He took them to the bottom of the garden, and came to the wild rose.

"I've got claws for you!" he said. "The witch Kirri did some strong magic. Look, here they are. I'll press each one into your stems, till you have claws all down them. Then I'll say a growing spell, and they will grow into you properly and belong to you."

So Cinder-Boy did that, and the wild rose felt the cat-claws growing firmly into the long stems.

"Now," said Cinder-Boy, in excitement, "now you will be able to climb up through the fruit-tree, wild rose. I will help you at first."

So Cinder-Boy took the wild rose stems, all set with claws, and pushed them up into the little fruit-tree that grew near by. The claws took hold of the bark and held on firmly. Soon all the stems were climbing up high through the little fruit tree, the claws digging themselves into the trunk and the branches.

The wild rose grew higher. It pulled itself up by its new claws. It was soon at the top of the wall! It could see right over it to the big world beyond.

"Now I'm happy!" said the wild rose to Cinder-Boy. "Come and sit up here on the wall beside me. Let us look at the big world together. Oh, Cinder-Boy, it is lovely up here. I am not shut in any longer. Thank you for my claws. I do hope I shall go on growing them now."

It did. And it grew beautiful scarlet berries in the autumn, for witch Kirri's winter bonnets. You should see how pretty they are when she trims them with the rosehips!

Ever since that day the wild roses have grown cats' claws all down their stems, sometimes green and sometimes red or pink. They use them to climb with. Have you seen them? If you haven't, do go and look. It will surprise you to see cats' claws growing out of a plant!

It was a good idea of Cinder-Boy's, wasn't it?

Mr
Squiggle

"Cathy, will you stop scribbling over everything?" said her mother. "Look here – you've made squiggles and scribbles on the kitchen wall – and I've found some silly squiggles on the door of the shed outside. Why do you do it?"

"Well, I can't write words properly yet," said Cathy, "and I'm not very good at drawing. So I just do squiggles – like this!"

And will you believe it, she took her pencil and did a squiggle on the nice clean tablecloth!

Her mother took her pencil away from her. "Very well – if you are as silly as all that, you shan't have a pencil!" she said.

But Cathy had got such a habit of

scribbling here, there and everywhere that she simply couldn't do without something in her fingers for scribbling. She found a blue crayon and began scribbling on the doorstep with it.

So her mother took that away, too. Then Cathy found a piece of white blackboard chalk, and dear me, the mess she made with that! There were squiggles on the garden gate and scribbles on the garden seat!

Even her father got angry. "Each time I find a squiggle, I shall smack your fingers," he said. "If *you* can't stop them scribbling, I will!"

"I do hope she won't grow up into one of those dreadful people who sign their names everywhere," said Mother. "I can't think why she does it – she doesn't even write words – it's just squiggles!"

Cathy didn't stop squiggling and scribbling. She got into trouble for it at school, too, because she scribbled all over the wall next to her seat in class.

"One of these days," said Miss Brown, the teacher, to Cathy, "you'll meet Mr Squiggle, who knows the language of squiggles – and, dear me, won't you be surprised at the nonsense you've written! You can't understand it, but he'll be able to!"

Cathy was certain that Miss Brown was joking, and she laughed. But will you believe it, the very next day she did meet Mr Squiggle!

She was going home from school. She had with her a piece of red chalk, and she was simply longing to scribble on something with it. When she came to one of the sheds belonging to Mr Straw, the farmer, she began to scribble all over it in red. It really looked horrid, and quite spoilt the shed.

And then she heard a squeaky voice behind her. "How dare you sign my name like that! I wondered who it was writing my name everywhere – and oh, my goodness, what naughty things you write – and then sign my name to them!"

Cathy turned round in surprise. She saw a thin little man bristling with pencils and pens and crayons. They were in rows of pockets, and he even had a row of red pencils in his hat, and some behind his ears. He looked rather like a brownie, she thought.

"I *don't* sign your name!" said Cathy, indignantly. "I don't even know it!"

"My name is Mr Squiggle," said the thin little man. "And look – here's my name. You've written it three times on this wall!"

He pointed to some funny little

squiggles. "See? That's my name – and that, and that. Watch while I sign it and you'll see it's really exactly like my signature."

He scribbled something with one of his pencils – and sure enough it was exactly like the three squiggles Cathy had made.

"Well, I didn't know I was signing your name," said Cathy. "It just looks like a squiggle to me."

"Well, it is. I told you my name was Squiggle, so, of course, it's a squiggle like that when I write it," said Mr Squiggle. "And let me tell you this – if some of the things you've said in the squiggle language get known, you'll be in very serious trouble."

"What things? I haven't written anything at all!" said Cathy in fright.

"Well, look here – see this?" said Mr Squiggle, pointing to a silly-looking squiggle that Cathy had done on the shed wall. "Do you know what that says in squiggle language? It says, 'I'll smack old witch Green-Eyes.' Fancy that! Suppose she came along and read that!"

"I didn't write that," said Cathy. "I don't even know witch Green-Eyes."

"Well, come along and see her," said Mr Squiggle, pulling at Cathy's arm. "Tell her you didn't mean to write that, so that if she sees it, she won't mind."

"No, thank you," Cathy said in alarm.

"And look here – see those squiggles?" said Mr Squiggle, pointing and suddenly looking very fierce. "You've actually written 'The goblin Long-Nose is always poking his nose into things. It wants pulling.' You're a very rude little girl. I've a good mind to bring Long-Nose here and show him what you've written about him."

"No, don't," said Cathy, almost in tears. "I tell you, I don't know him. Why should I write things about people I don't know?"

"Just part of your silliness, I suppose,"

said Mr Squiggle "I passed through your garden yesterday and what did I see written on your garden seat?"

"What?" asked Cathy, in fright.

"I saw, 'All fairies must keep out of this garden or I'll stamp on their toes'!" said Mr Squiggle. "That's a nasty, unkind thing to write!"

Cathy was full of horror. "Did I really write that in squiggle language? I didn't know I had. Oh, I don't want the fairies to keep out of my garden. I'm longing to see one."

"Well, you won't now," said Mr Squiggle, taking out a big rubber and beginning to rub out some of Cathy's silly squiggles. "Not one will come near you. You're a rude little girl!"

"I'm *not*! I didn't know what I was writing!" wept Cathy. "Have I said anything else dreadful?"

"Good gracious me, yes," said Mr Squiggle, rubbing out hard. "There was one thing I had to rub out at once, in case you got the Jumping Imps after you. You'd written it on your school

playground. You wrote, 'If ever I catch a Jumping Imp I'll slap him and put him in the dustbin.' Fancy being so rude. If I hadn't rubbed that out at once, you'd have had dozens of Jumping Imps giving *you* a few slaps!"

"Was it you who rubbed out what I'd chalked in the playground, then?" said

Cathy. "I thought the rain had washed it away."

"I couldn't wait for the rain," said Mr Squiggle. "It had to be rubbed out at once. You give me a dreadful lot of work. All this rubbing out of rude squiggle messages! I tell you, you'll get into serious trouble one day, writing in the squiggle language! Instead of going round after you and rubbing out, I'll fetch someone like witch Green-Eyes and let her read what you've written. Then she'll be after you."

"I won't write in the squiggle language any more," said Cathy. "Never, never, never. It's dreadful to write rude things without meaning to."

Mr Squiggle rubbed out the very last scribble. He put his rubber back into his pocket. "I've heard your mother telling you to stop," he said. "And you don't. Look – I'm going to write something in the squiggle language now – watch me!"

And he wrote a lot of quick scribbles. "See what I've written?" he said. "'Cathy is a rude girl. Give her a smack whenever you go by. Signed, Mr Squiggle'!"

Then, before Cathy could say another word, he raised his hat to her, making all the pencils in it click together, jumped over the hedge and completely disappeared.

Cathy stared at the squiggles he had written neatly on the shed wall. Did they really mean what he had said? She didn't want to get sly slaps wherever she went! And then, quite suddenly, she felt a sharp little slap on her leg, and someone laughed a high laugh like a blackbird.

But there was no one to be seen. Cathy turned to the shed wall. She took out her hanky, wetted it in a nearby rain-barrel, and began to rub out what Mr Squiggle had written. No more slaps for her!

She didn't get any more slaps – and neither did she scribble any more squiggles. Are you a scribbler, too? Just be careful you don't write something rude without meaning to!

Clever Old
Green-Eyes

Green-Eyes belonged to Morris. She was a big black cat, with a thick, silky coat, and the greenest eyes you ever saw.

"They are as green as the cucumbers you buy in the summer, Mummy," said Morris. "I do love Green-Eyes. She purrs so loudly, and she loves sitting on my knee. She is the nicest cat in the world."

Morris bought Green-Eyes a lovely Christmas present. It was a cat-basket made of wicker. Morris begged an old cushion from his mother, and an old bit of blanket. Then he picked up Green-Eyes and sat her down in the basket.

"It's yours, Green-Eyes, with my love," said Morris. "Mummy, may I have Green-Eyes's basket in my bedroom, please? Do let me. She is very good, and she

161

won't make my room untidy or smelly at
all, I promise you."

Well, Mother didn't very much like a
cat sleeping in Morris's room, but
certainly Green-Eyes was a very good,
quiet cat – so she said yes.

And, in great delight, Morris carried
the basket up to his own little bedroom,
with Green-Eyes following at his heels.

"There," he said to Green-Eyes, "you
can sleep in my bedroom every night

now, Green-Eyes – you in your basket and I in my bed. I will always leave the window open a little way so that you can come in and out as you want to. You can easily scramble up the tree outside and come in through the window, if you are not in your basket when I have to go to bed."

Green-Eyes was delighted. She purred loudly. "Thank you, Morris. It is a very lovely basket and I like it very much. You are a kind little boy."

For three or four months Green-Eyes slept in her basket in Morris's bedroom – and then one morning Morris gave such a yell of surprise and delight that his mother came running to see what was the matter.

"Mummy, oh Mummy! Green-Eyes has got four tiny little kittens in her basket! Oh, Mummy, we've got kittens. Isn't it exciting?"

"Very exciting," said Mother. "But Green-Eyes will have to go to the barn now, Morris. I can't have five cats in your bedroom."

"Oh, Mummy – but four of them are only tiny kittens!" said Morris, almost in tears. "Mummy, Green-Eyes is so used to sleeping in my room now – she loves it. Don't make her unhappy by turning her out just when she's got four dear little kittens to look after. They will be safe with me. The rats might get them out in the barn."

"Dear me, Green-Eyes will certainly see that they don't!" said Mother. "She has killed a good many rats in her time. No, Morris dear – she and her kittens must go to the barn. There is plenty of straw there to make her a nice soft bed. She will be very happy there."

"She will miss me so at night," said Morris. "And I shall miss her, too."

But Morris's mother was quite firm about it. Green-Eyes had got to go to the barn with all her kittens, and go she did. Mother picked up the kittens, which squealed loudly. She went downstairs with them and Green-Eyes followed at once.

Mother took the four tiny kittens to

the barn. They were all as black as could be, just like Green-Eyes, and one of them had tiny white feet.

Green-Eyes made a bed for them in the straw and lay down. Mother gave her the kittens and they nestled up to her, asking her for some milk. Green-Eyes purred loudly.

"There, you see!" said Mother to Morris. "Green-Eyes is quite happy."

But when night-time came and Morris looked at the empty basket, he felt sure that Green-Eyes wasn't at all happy. Then he heard a little soft jump, and there was Green-Eyes in his bedroom, looking up at him.

"Oh, Green-Eyes – are you missing me? Are you missing your basket?" said Morris. "Mummy doesn't want your nice basket out in the barn. She says straw will be all right for you and the kittens. Let me stroke you. There now, go back to your kittens, and don't be miserable because you've been turned out!"

The kittens grew well, out in the barn. Their eyes opened and were very blue. Morris's mother said they would turn green later on. Soon they were able to creep out of the straw and play about a little. Morris loved them – but he still wished he could have them indoors!

One night about four weeks after the kittens had been born, Morris woke with a jump. His window was shut, and something was knocking against it. *Thud, thud, thud,* went the knocking, very soft and slow. He opened the window and Green-Eyes jumped inside, carrying a kitten by the skin at the back of its neck, the way all mother-cats carry their kittens. She dropped it into the basket nearby, gave a tiny mew, and then sprang out of the window and climbed down the tree.

Morris was astonished. "Green-Eyes! What are you doing? Why have you brought your kitten here?"

Soon the cat was back with yet another kitten. Morris was more astonished than ever. What could Green-Eyes be doing? Was she tired of the barn? Had she suddenly taken it into her head to bring her kittens to the place that she herself liked so much? It was all very puzzling.

Then Morris smelled something funny – smoke! He sniffed and sniffed. Yes – it was smoke. But what smoke could it be? There was no bonfire burning, he knew that.

He slipped downstairs just as Green-Eyes jumped in at the window with her third kitten in her mouth. He ran out of the back door and went to the barn. Smoke was coming out of it!

"Fire! Fire!" yelled Morris. "Mummy! Daddy! The barn's on fire! Quick, quick!"

He saw Green-Eyes come out of the smoking barn, dragging her last kitten in her mouth.

"Oh, you good, clever little cat!" he

said. "You have saved all your kittens by yourself! And perhaps you will have saved our barn, too, if only Mummy and Daddy come quickly enough."

It wasn't very long before a crowd of grown-ups were hosing the smoking barn with water. Inside, fast asleep, was an old tramp. He had lit a candle there and fallen asleep without putting it out. It had burned down, set the straw alight, and set fire to the big barn.

Soon the fire was out. The tramp was rubbing his eyes in amazement, and Morris was telling everyone about Green-Eyes.

"She brought her kittens to my bedroom, where her old basket is, and that's what woke me. I went out and saw the barn on fire. Mummy, Daddy, Green-Eyes saved the barn – and saved the life of that old tramp, too!"

They all went back to bed, happy and excited. Mother peeped into Morris's room and smiled.

"Well, well, I suppose I'll have to let you have Green-Eyes and all the kittens there now, Morris. She saved our barn for us, so I must give her a reward!"

So Green-Eyes slept in the basket with her four kittens, and Morris was very

happy. But when they were six weeks old they woke him up every morning by clambering on to his bed and nibbling his nose. So, in the end, he had to take them down to the kitchen!

"As soon as they go to their new homes you can come back to my bedroom and sleep in your basket," he told Green-Eyes. "You'll like that, won't you?"

"Purrrrr-rrr-rrr," said Green-Eyes, and Morris knew what *that* meant.

The Two Bad Boys

There were once two bad boys called Tom and Jim. They were not truthful and they were not honest – in fact, they stole apples from outside shops, and once Tom had taken a full milk-bottle from a doorstep!

This was really dreadful. The apples were green and gave them both a pain, and Tom fell with the milk-bottle, broke it, and cut his hand, so they didn't get any good out of their stealing; but how sad their mothers were to know they had children like that!

"Nobody gets happiness out of badness," said Tom's mother, as she bandaged his hand.

Tom didn't believe her – but when he found that the Sunday school party was to be held on Saturday and that he and

Jim were not invited, be began to wish he hadn't been so bad!

He grumbled about it to Jim. "There's going to be crackers and balloons and blow-up pigs that squeak, and all kinds of goodies and oranges and sweets and a toy for everybody!" he said. "I wish we were going."

"Well!" said Jim. "What about creeping in before the party begins and taking a few things for ourselves? We could easily do that. We could creep in at a window."

Jim was a very bad boy as you can see. Tom nodded his head. "All right," he said. "We will. Let's go and peep in at the window on Friday and see what sort of toys are there."

So on Friday they peeped in at the window. They saw Mrs Jones and Miss Brown arranging everything ready for the next day. They saw the dishes of sweets put out, the plates of oranges. There were no cakes or buns yet, because they would be made next day. They saw the big balloons being blown up, and watched the balloon-pigs being stood all

down the table for the children.

There was a big table for the toys too.
My goodness, what lovely toys! There
were two big humming-tops, a train
that could whistle, a doll that could say
"Ma-ma, Pa-pa", some tiny motor-cars
with little hooters, a bear that growled, a
monkey that squeaked – oh, more toys
than Tom and Jim could count.

They watched until Mrs Jones and Miss Brown put the light out and went away. Then the boys spoke to one another.

"We'll come tomorrow, when the windows will be opened to air the room – and we'll take oranges, sweets, balloons, crackers and toys!"

They slipped away, thinking nobody had heard them. But the toys had both seen and heard them! They knew Tom and Jim all right! Everybody knew about those two bad boys.

"Did you hear what they said?" cried the bear, in excitement. "We won't let them steal us! We'll give them such a fright!"

So when the next night came, and the two naughty boys crept in at an open window, the toys were ready. The monkey had taken three of the balloon-pigs from the table, and he and the doll and the bear pulled the little corks from the pigs' mouths as soon as the boys came in.

You know what noise a balloon-pig makes when the air goes out of him,

don't you? "Eeeeeeeeeeeeeeeeee!" they all said in their mournful voices. "Eeeeeeeeeeeeeee!"

Tom and Jim stood still in fright. Whatever was that? The pigs stopped making a noise and fell over, quite flat. Then the teddy bear pressed himself in the middle.

"Grrrrrrrrr!" he said. "Grrrrrrrrrr!"

"Ooooh!" said Tom and Jim. "Is it a dog growling!"

"Grrrrrrrrr!" said the bear again, quite enjoying himself. Then the monkey and the other toys took the three humming-tops and set them spinning madly on the floor. They all hummed like enormous bees! "Zoooooooooom! Zeeeeeeeeeeeem! Zooooooooom!" they went. Tom tried to run away and he fell over a mat that caught his foot. *Bang!*

"Ow!" cried Tom. "Something's caught me! What's making that noise? Are we in a beehive? I wish we could see, but the room's all dark!"

The monkey pressed himself in the middle and made loud squeaks. "Eeoo,

eeoo, eeoo, eeoo!" Jim fell over Tom in a fright. The monkey nearly laughed out loud!

Then the engine of the train began to whistle. "Pheeeeeeeeeeeee!" it went, as loudly as it could. Good gracious, what a fright it gave the two bad boys! They could hardly get up!

"Where's the window? Where's the window?" cried Jim.

Now the talking doll began to call, "Mama, Papa, Mama, Papa!" at the top of her voice, and the monkey and bear pressed the little hooters of the motor-cars at the same time.

"Honk, honk, honk! Honk, Mama, Papa, honk, honk, Mama, honk, Papa, honk!" What a noise! Tom and Jim rushed for the window and tried to climb through – and then the monkey had a bright idea. He took the brooch off his coat and drove the pin into a big balloon hanging near him.

BANG! It went off with such a loud pop that even the toys were startled. Jim and Tom fell to the ground.

179

"I'm shot!" groaned Tom.

"So am I!" cried Jim. "Somebody's shot us. Didn't you hear the bang!"

And there they lay groaning, thinking they were shot, till the door opened and in trooped all the children who had been invited to the party! How surprised they were to see Tom and Jim – and you may be sure they guessed at once what those two bad boys had come for!

They shooed them out of the door, they laughed at them – and they banged the door behind them. Tom and Jim began to cry. How they wished they could go and join the happy children in the room, with all the balloons and toys!

"It's our own fault," said Tom, wiping his eyes. "Mum says nobody gets any happiness out of being bad. I'm going to be good for a change. I've had a real fright tonight, and I'm going home to find out where I've been shot!"

Well, he won't find where he's shot, and neither will Jim – but the toys will have done a good deed if they have stopped those two boys from being bad. The monkey still laughs when he remembers all that happened that evening!

Buttons and
Bows

"You're lazy, Janie," said her mother. "You're over six years old and you can't tie a bow or do up your buttons properly yet!"

"Well, there's always someone who will do them up for me," said Janie.

"So I suppose you think you need never learn, and you'll grow up to be an old woman who runs round the world asking people to do up her shoes and tie her apron strings for her!" said her mother. "I'm ashamed of you."

"I shall wear shoes without buttons or bows, and I shan't wear an apron when I grow up," said Janie. She just didn't mean to learn things that were a nuisance!

"I'll teach you," said John-from-next-door. He had been to borrow a book, and he had heard all this.

"Thank you, John, that's kind of you," said Janie's mother.

But Janie turned away. "No, thank you," she said. "I'm busy just now. I have to practise my skipping."

"You don't have to," called John. "You're just making an excuse!"

Now the next day John went to the woods to find blackberries. Janie saw him going and called, "I'm coming with you. I want some blackberries, too."

"Well, you can come – but you can pick your own blackberries," said John. "And if your shoe comes undone you can do it up yourself, and if your hair-ribbon comes untied you can tie that, too. I'm not going to do things for you, lazy little Janie."

"I don't care," said Janie. "I shall get someone else to do them, that's all."

She went off with John. She liked him, although he wouldn't run round after her as the other children often did. "Poor little Janie!" they would say. "She's only little – she can't do this, she can't do that – we'll do it for her!"

But John wouldn't. "My five-year-old sister can tie bows and do up buttons and even do up hooks and eyes," he said. "And she can sew, too. Why shouldn't Janie?"

He and Janie were soon in the wood. It was a big wood, and the trees grew thickly here and there, but now and again there were clear spaces where great masses of blackberry brambles grew. And, oh, the blackberries there! They were bigger and juicier than anywhere else.

The two children were soon busy picking and eating. And then a surprising thing happened.

Something pulled at John's shorts, and a small, high voice spoke a few quick words to him. John looked down, alarmed and surprised.

He was even more surprised when he saw what was pulling at his shorts! It was a small goblin with bright green eyes and big, pointed ears!

"Boy! Listen to me! Can you help me for a minute?" said the goblin's strange, high voice.

"Good gracious – who are you?" said John. "Hi, Janie, look here – what do you suppose it is? A goblin?"

"Oh!" squealed Janie. "Yes, it must be. Or perhaps a brownie. No, brownies have beards. What are you, little man, and what do you want?"

The goblin went to her, smiling. "I didn't see you," he said, "or I would have asked you to help me! You'd be better than a boy. I'm a goblin, and I'm just off to an important meeting with the King of the Goblins."

"Are you really?" said Janie, amazed. "Goodness me, a goblin – this is very extraordinary. I've never seen a real goblin before."

"You wouldn't see me now if I hadn't wanted you to," said the goblin. "But I'm in a real fix and I had to ask someone to help me."

"What is it you want?" said Janie.

"Just wait a minute and I'll show you,"

said the goblin. He ran to a nearby bank, opened a little green door there and disappeared. He came out again almost at once, bringing with him a lovely red tunic and a pair of pointed shoes with long green laces.

"Look," he said. "I have to wear these to go to the meeting. My aunt usually helps me to dress, because the tunic buttons all the way up the back and I can't reach to do the buttons up. And my shoes have to lace all the way up my legs and tie in a bow behind my knees. Well, of course I can do up buttons as well as anyone and tie laces too – but nobody can do those things behind themselves very well."

He stopped and looked at Janie. "So would you please do up the buttons for me and lace up the shoes round my leg and tie the bows behind my knees?" he asked.

Janie shook her head. "Good gracious, no. I couldn't do up buttons as little as that. I can't even do up big buttons properly. And I couldn't possibly lace those things up your legs and tie bows. I don't know how to."

"Well! And you're a girl, too!" said the goblin, in disgust. "I don't believe you. Every girl can do things like that. You don't want to! You're a spoilsport!"

"I'll do them for you if you like," said John. "Put on your tunic and the shoes and I'll do my best to do them up."

The goblin put on his tunic and his shoes, and then stood with his back to

John. John had quite a job to do up all the buttons! There were sixty-two of them, very small indeed, but he managed all right.

Then he looped the laces round the goblin's legs and tied them into neat bows at the back of his knees.

"There you are," he said. "All done! You look very nice!"

"Thank you very much indeed!" said the goblin, and he ran off in delight. "I'll send you a reward some time!"

"Well, I'm glad I couldn't do up buttons or tie bows," said Janie, when he had gone. "I would have hated to do up so many."

But she didn't feel like that when she saw how the goblin rewarded John. He sent him an invitation to his birthday party!

Please do come, he wrote. *There will be everything you like best to eat, and there will be a present-tree growing presents for every guest. You just wish and pick your present off the tree! And will you bring a friend with you? But not that nasty little girl who wouldn't help me. Somebody nice. It's at midnight on the next full-moon night.*

Happy wishes from
Humpy the Goblin.

"Oh, take me, take me, John, please, please do!" begged Janie when John showed her the letter. But John shook his head.

"Of course I can't, Janie. You must have seemed very horrid to him. He really couldn't believe that a little girl couldn't do such simple things. You'd better begin learning straight away, in case you miss some other treat!"

So Janie is busy learning to do up buttons and tie bows and do up hooks and eyes as well – just in case! I hope you'll teach your small brothers and sisters what to do with buttons and bows – you just never know when things will come in useful, do you?